THE LAND OF NO REFLECTION

ANITHA KRISHNAN

DREAM PEDLAR BOOKS

Ebook ISBN: 978-1-7388158-5-2

Paperback ISBN: 978-1-7388158-6-9

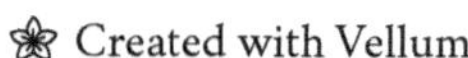 Created with Vellum

ABOUT THIS BOOK

The Land of No Reflection

You don't need eyes, let alone a mirror, to peer into the depths of your own soul.

Sight is a privilege denied to everyone by law in the land of Parinara. Every child is blindfolded at birth. Even the dead are buried blindfolded. To see is an unpardonable crime, punishable by death.

Yet, fifteen-year-old Viola indulges in a momentary curiosity and violates the law, only to find that the gift of sight comes at an exorbitant price.

To look outward, she must first lose sight of what lies inward. But therein lie the secrets that even sightlessness cannot conceal.

For Kala Maami,
I miss you. I hope the Gods realize how lucky they are to have you in their midst.

For Dhruv,
you are the reason I journeyed back to my true self.

For Abhinav,
you showed me that all it takes to change is a simple willingness to learn.

I love you both more than words can ever convey.

CHAPTER 1

THE GREAT ESCAPE

"How much longer?" Viola whined, stumbling over a muddy terrain littered with small rocks.

Her fingers itched to rub her cheekbones, where the blindfold she wore chafed her skin. But her hands were cuffed and tied with a leash of cotton rope, the other end looped around her sister's wrist.

No way could Viola pull her hands close to her face and slip her fingers under the blindfold to soothe her scraped skin with a satisfying rub without earning a cuff on her ear.

Besides, it was this very kind of transgression that had landed her hands in cuffs and a leash to begin with. For in the land of Parinara, where even the dead were buried blindfolded, the living could certainly not have it any other way.

"Soon enough," Talia replied. "Sooner, if you quit whining."

Which meant Talia was clueless too. And what Viola had suspected all along was true.

"We're running away then, aren't we?" Viola made no effort to keep the accusation out of her tone.

She stumbled into Talia who had stopped abruptly.

Affronted by Viola's words, no doubt. Viola gleaned a whit of satisfaction from the power she could wield over her sister in this petty, childish way. A precise selection of words, delivered with just the right hint of accusation. A charge of wrongdoing. That was all it took to get Talia to stop and turn all her attention towards her only sibling.

Viola drew in her breath, ready to face Talia's reaction, when she was yanked off her feet and thrown to one side. She fell into what felt like a bush. Spindly twigs and thorns scraped her arms.

Two hands—her sister's, she assumed, even hoped—slid under her armpits and dragged her a few feet on the muddy ground, then propped her up against a tree trunk.

Instinctively, she rubbed her face against it. Rough and scaly. Deep ridges. An oak tree.

She patted the ground around her with her hands, not stopping until she found an acorn and clutched it in her palm like a talisman, something to hold on to until the danger had passed.

Talia's hand, rough and calloused yet softer than the oak's bark, pressed down on her mouth, and Viola stifled a scream with the skill of someone who had had ample practice in doing so.

The horses were still several miles away, but Talia had heard them. Her mind must have been empty, free of the clatter of thoughts. Viola could hear them now, a feeble clunk of hooves, fainter than the thumping of her heart. She could only hope that the sounds of their attempt to hide had gone unnoticed.

The breeze was blowing their way, she noticed only a moment later as she withdrew from her mind and settled into her body. It was unlikely the riders would have heard them. They had gotten lucky.

The earth was warm, but her breath was cool. It was evening. Only a few more hours of daylight left.

"It is not a crime to seek safety," Talia whispered into Viola's ear. "Whether we get it by staying put or by running away." There was no anger in her voice. Only sadness. And a tired resignation.

A deep sense of shame and guilt swelled from somewhere deep within Viola. Tears flowed down her cheeks, stinging where her skin was bruised, and plopped audibly on her skirt. It was all her fault. She should never have let Ronin get under her skin.

But when the boys were teasing her on the playground, daring her to do the unforgivable, she hadn't really tried hard to resist. Besides, she had wanted to determine whether Ronin was more beautiful in person than the image she had concocted of him in her mind.

With a strange thrill bolting up her spine, Viola had untied her blindfold and looked at him. And he had done the same. Opened his eyes and let his gaze settle upon her.

Even though it was the most outrageous crime one could ever commit in the land of Parinara. The only crime for which immediate death by guillotine was the only punishment.

But she had fancied him after all. And he had fancied her.

Not anymore, though. For whatever he had seen in her eyes when she had removed her blindfold had first paralyzed him, then sent him scuttling backwards, and he and his friends had run away from her as if to stand in her vicinity was to invite trouble. And he hadn't even told her why.

But Talia had understood. And she had panicked. And she

had hastily gathered two apples and a handful of almonds in a handkerchief, no larger than her hands put together, slid a dagger into her boot, tightened the blindfold around her sister's eyes, and run into the woods with her sister on a leash. And they had run all night and all day, not stopping even once, until now.

"What did Ronin look like?" Talia asked in a whisper.

"Uglier than dung."

Talia's body shook as she burst into laughter but refused to lend sound to it. A nightingale trilled in the branches above, joining in their mirth.

"Good riddance of bad rubbish then," Talia said at last, then sank against the trunk of the tree.

Viola leaned into her, slipped a hand into her sister's, and the two were compelled to squander several precious minutes of daylight, pinned to their spot under the tree, taking soft, shallow breaths, hoping against hope the riders would thunder down the trail without noticing their presence.

Whoever said that the truth shall set you free had been wrong. The absence of vision had been a blessing in more ways than one.

Viola could hear the horses in the distance. The earth beneath her vibrated under their thundering hooves. When they came closer, she'd even be able to tell whom they belonged to from a mere whiff of the oils in their coats.

She thought she had known what Ronin looked like not because she had ever seen him but because she had often run her fingers over his face, memorized every slant and slope, and conjured up an image of the guy she had hoped to marry next summer when she turned sixteen.

She had even known his irises would be a ghostly white,

like hers, like Talia's, like that of all the children born in Parinara within the last three decades. This was a fact, albeit one that couldn't be verified without breaking the law.

Blindfolded at birth, before they had even had a chance to open their honey-golden eyes for the first time, they had all slipped out from one dark womb into another. Larger. Colder. More treacherous. None of them had ever seen the world around them.

What Viola had not accounted for, or even considered the likelihood of, had been the cruelty etched on Ronin's face. It had lain hidden in the corners of his mouth that turned down, in the slight upturn of his nose, and in the way he held his head so high he was looking down on her. Although he had been a good inch shorter.

Yes. Talia was right. Good riddance of bad rubbish indeed.

A sigh escaped her lips.

Wrong move.

"There!" A voice boomed so loudly it ricocheted off the trees and the sisters couldn't tell where it had come from. Which is what the caller had intended.

He was a soldier, it was evident. Of senior standing. A captain. It was in the way he had called out. Issued his command.

It was the faint whiff of their musky scent and the strong leathery odour of their saddles that told her the horses came from the Queen's stables. Only Her Majesty's horses had such a rich scent. Only the most important men had been sent to capture her and Talia. But how many, she couldn't yet discern.

Viola held her breath and strained her ears. Silence pressed upon her like a burial shroud. Even the birds held their breath, afraid of giving themselves away. The soldier, or soldiers, were doing the same, she knew.

Blindfolded. Just as she was. As Talia was. As every inhabitant of Parinara had been for the last three decades.

Without the advantage of sight to rely on, their remaining senses had been sharpened to excruciating heights, as if every pore on their skin was now a tiny eye that had to take in every scent and sound in their vicinity, record the movement of every shadow, show them everything they would never have discerned with open eyes.

Which is how Viola noticed something slithering stealthily somewhere above her. Noiseless. Yet disturbing the air with its very movement, a perturbation that she had been looking for. Talia had noticed it too. She gave Viola's hand a tiny squeeze.

Like a thick coil of rope unfurling, the slithering creature glided over and down Viola's left shoulder, wound its way around her hip and down her leg. Another moment, and it would kiss the ground and rustle through the woodland, the soft swish of its motion cleaving the silence like a cannon shot.

Viola withdrew her hand from her sister's grasp, grabbed the creature by its tail, pivoted on her right foot and flung the deadly reptile in the general direction of where she expected the Queen's soldiers had positioned themselves.

A cry of shock proved her calculation was right. Shouts and neighs rent the air and shredded the world around them into countless pieces. There were four horses in all, she could now hear. But only three riders.

And then the scream she had been hoping for. The cobra had bitten one of the horses.

In the mayhem that ensued, Talia spun and launched her dagger in the direction of the voice that issued commands. The hiss of the blade piercing the air grabbed the captain's attention a moment too late. He turned around to block and deflect the weapon, but it caught him square in the heart.

"Run!" Talia hissed.

Viola and Talia ran deeper into the woods, mapping out an entire path ahead of them simply by the way the breeze, still in their favour, flowed around and revealed where the trees stood so the girls could evade the obstacles.

For another night they ran, linked by a leash, not knowing where they were going, yet not daring to stop, until the grass beneath their boots morphed into something hard and uneven. Brick. Or cobblestone, perhaps.

All they knew was that in two nights and one day, they had come farther than they had ever travelled in their lives of fifteen years.

CHAPTER 2
LOOK INTO MY EYES

"Halt! Who goes there?"

A tentative voice. A young lad's.

Footsteps. Hesitant. But determined. As if to prove something.

The clang of body armour. The rhythmic thunk of a spear hitting the ground like a walking stick. A new recruit, perhaps. Likely overzealous in discharging his duties.

"Parinaryans?" Incredulity in his voice. The wretched, cursed ones from the land of the blindfolded. Their reputation had preceded them.

But no one expected Parinaryans, the people of Parinara, to travel far from their homes. The young were blindfolded at birth. The ones who had lived long enough to enjoy the gift of sight had long forgotten what the world had looked like in the olden days.

"Parinaryans? Speak up!"

Uncertainty. This was unfamiliar territory for him. Also, a hint of annoyance. Fear. He was afraid. Of what two Parinaryans, so far away from their homeland, could be capable of.

The fear in his voice reminded Viola of Ronin, of the way she had hoped to see desire in his eyes for her but had found fear and disgust instead.

"We're not from Parinara," Talia said. It was evident Viola wouldn't be supplying the requisite words for now. "We come from the mountains beyond the northern border of Parinara. The Mountains of the Seers. We were told we wouldn't be permitted to cross the land of Parinara unless we were blindfolded."

Talia was spinning a tale and Viola hoped that her sister at least had the faintest idea how that story would end.

"How will I know you're speaking the truth?" Clearly, a new recruit. A more seasoned guard would have dragged the sisters to his captain without having engaged in conversation with them. Nor would he have accosted them single-handedly.

"With your permission, I can remove my blindfold and show you," Talia offered. "My eyes are as golden and shiny as I presume yours are, Sir."

A soft rustle and a sigh. Quaking quagmires! Talia was being a tease. She had bobbed a curtsy to him.

"The people of this land are blessed with ocean-green eyes," the soldier said with a smirk.

Viola braced herself for what was about to happen. Talia took her time to remove the blindfold. Viola pictured her sister standing in front of the guard, eyes closed, demure, hesitant as a bride, longing to be unveiled, yet reluctant to demonstrate her desire.

In one swift moment, Talia popped her eyes open.

"Aaaah!" The young soldier yelled and staggered back at

the sight of Talia's eyes, surely white as blanched almonds, her irises obliterated by disuse.

His spear fell to the ground beside him. Viola sprung forward and landed a kick on his chest. He fell back limply, likely rendered unconscious from shock. Viola's blow had been unnecessary.

Viola turned back to Talia and touched her face. She had blindfolded herself once more.

"Let's hide before more of them turn up," Talia whispered and pulled Viola behind her and up a tree.

An apple tree. Luck was in their favour. The two apples and the handkerchief full of almonds that Talia had packed when the sisters set out from Parinara with unceremonious haste had long disappeared from their possession.

Several minutes passed before the fallen guard was discovered. Several more minutes passed before what the sisters presumed was a little army came marching down and positioned themselves right below their tree.

"This is where our comrade was found robbed of his consciousness," a voice announced. "Scour the woods for the reprobates who are guilty of this. Two young Parinaryan women, our confrère revealed when he came to his senses. You have until sundown. Tomorrow morning, His Highness, Prince Alahaid, will lead us to Parinara to return their criminals to their land."

Prince Alahaid. They were in Anansia, Parinara's neighbour to the south.

The guards, there must have been about a score of them, saluted their captain, their armour and weapons clanging in unison, and ran off in four different directions, causing the earth to tremble under the rhythmic march of their feet, without sparing a single glance heavenwards.

"War will be upon us soon," Talia said, her mouth full of apple.

"Her Majesty has no one but herself to blame," Viola said. It was a satisfactory thought. Because it had all begun with the Queen of Parinara.

CHAPTER 3

MIRROR, MIRROR ON THE WALL

Three decades ago, eighteen-year-old Princess Sahana of Parinara, had been in search of a suitor who would marry her and ascend the throne after the death of her ailing father.

She had hoped to marry King Janaheed, ruler of the Kingdom of Anansia, Parinara's neighbour to the south. But the renowned King had sought betrothal to another.

Impatient as the young princess had been, she had peered into the largest mirror in her bedroom and demanded it reveal her future husband. The mirror had presented only a cloud of smoke.

She had walked up to every mirror in her palace and posed the same question over and over again.

"You with a back of hard steel
and a face of shiny glass,
Reveal
who will have the good fortune
of marrying me at last!"

And every time she had received a cloud of smoke in response.

Exasperated, she trekked to the mountains beyond the northern borders of her land to consult the Seers. None granted her an audience for nine days.

On the tenth day, an old woman took pity on the young princess, stubborn if somewhat misguided, and said, "The mirrors do not believe marriage to you will bring good fortune to any man."

Those were the last words the old woman spoke, for the princess drew her sword from her scabbard and beheaded the unfortunate old hag who had dared speak the truth.

News of the old Seer's verdict and her death reached Parinara long before Princess Sahana returned home to discover that she was now Queen Sahana, her ailing father having died the instant he had received word of his daughter's cruelty, and that her subjects now regarded her with a mixture of fear and pity.

She peered into the mirror in her bedroom and demanded,

> *"You with a back of hard steel*
> *and a face of shiny glass,*
> *Reveal*
> *who will marry me at last!"*

Without hesitation, the mirror said,

> *"No human is so condemned,*
> *no devil is so wretched,*
> *to be wedded to a heart*
> *as cold and cruel as yours."*

Queen Sahana dealt with the matter the way she addressed every problem she ever encountered. A matter of mere obliteration.

Every mirror in the palace was taken down and destroyed, its glass pulverized, its metal thrown into a furnace.

When Queen Sahana saw her own face scowling back at her from the surface of the lake beside her palace, she had tall walls built around it.

When she saw her own reflection in the eyes of her advisors, she ruled that every Parinaryan's eyes be gouged out.

No amount of pleading or coaxing could bring Her Majesty to change her mind, until someone pointed out that a kingdom of blind subjects was extremely susceptible to invasion. Queen Sahana saw merit in that argument and consented to blindfolds instead of blindness.

For thirty years, Parinaryans have had little use for the sense of sight. Children born ever since the Queen's decree had not once seen the blue of the sky or the green of the trees, the honey-gold of their mothers' eyes or the beauty of their own little beings. Colours held no meaning for them.

But where their vision had dimmed, their hearing had sharpened and so had their intellect. They could tell a rose apart from a peony simply by their scents.

When they touched another being or object, they could *see* its shape and texture in their mind's eyes. They could know it and understand it better than they would have had they merely seen it.

CHAPTER 4

THE TRUTH ABOUT REFLECTIONS

"Does the Queen wear a blindfold?" Viola asked.

Talia did not reply at first. Had she fallen asleep? But her breath was not entirely relaxed, which suggested she was awake. Thinking.

"She has no reason to," Talia said. "Her Majesty does not want others to behold her. Nothing stops her from looking at them. Besides, how would we ever find out?"

"Nothing stops us from seeing each other now," Viola said with a frisson of excitement.

Talia gasped. The very idea was so foreign, so utterly incomprehensible, it had probably never occurred to her before.

But Viola, who had readily pulled out her blindfold when Ronin had dared her to yield a glimpse of her eyes, windows into her soul—her truth, he had teased—found the prospect of seeing her sister for the first time both exciting and daunting.

Viola had already formed an image of Talia in her head. As much as she wanted to know if Talia looked anything like it, she was also terrified to find out that she might not. What if

Talia looked sterner or less friendly than Viola knew her to be? She wouldn't be able to unsee if she didn't like what she'd see.

But Talia was already removing her blindfold, and Viola felt compelled to follow suit. The idea had been hers, after all.

"Wow," Talia said. "You're so gorgeous, little sister."

Coaxed by Talia's admiration, Viola opened her eyes. All the light of the world tried to seep into her eyes all at once, as if to compensate for a lifetime of absence. It stung. Viola squeezed her eyes shut. Only a few moments, and her eyelids fluttered open.

And she saw her sister for the first time. And her sister was everything she had known her to be. Lovely. Kind. Beautiful.

Viola knew a lot of words of description without knowing what they meant. White eyes, not unlike Ronin's. Is that what Viola's eyes looked like too? But Talia's eyes were not scary. Wonder why Ronin had been aghast at the sight of Viola's eyes?

"Wow, look at that." Talia held an apple out in front of her. Everything was a novelty to behold.

So, *this* is red, Viola thought. And *this* is green, she concluded as she ran her fingers over the leaves. She looked up at the sky. Blue? She wondered, but she wasn't certain for she knew that an overcast sky was grey.

"Oh no!" Talia said suddenly, pointing over Viola's shoulder to a large body of water in the distance.

"What? What's wrong?"

Talia didn't answer. She pressed her lips in grim thought. She cocked her head to one side and said to herself, "I wonder..."

Without warning, she hastily clambered down the tree,

pausing only once to slide her hand out of the leash, severing the fabric connection between the sisters.

"Wait for me!" Viola scrambled down after her.

Talia paid no heed but ran ahead and dove into the water, disappearing under the surface.

Viola screamed. She ran harder and reached the edge of the lake but did not jump in.

They had grown up blindfolded, but they hadn't been raised ignorant. Everybody knew it was dangerous to jump into a body of water if you didn't know how to swim. And Viola didn't. Neither did Talia, for that matter.

Viola looked where Talia had disappeared, but the surface was calm. Not even a ripple. The sun formed a perfect reflection in the water.

Viola called out to her sister repeatedly, her eyes trained on the spot where Talia had jumped in.

"Psst!" A whisper startled her.

Viola spun around, but no one was in sight.

"Psst!" The sound came from somewhere behind her.

She turned back to face the lake. Nothing.

"Look down!" the voice whispered.

And there she was. Talia. Looking up at Viola. Only, her eyes were no longer white. Her irises were green as the leaves of the apple tree.

Relieved and angry all at once, Viola hissed, "What are you doing in there? Come out now before we are seen or caught."

Talia laughed. "I can't," she said. "This is where I belong."

"What do you mean?"

"Don't you get it? I am you. And you are me."

"You're making no sense," Viola said. She looked around frantically. Seeking aid. Bracing for danger. There were no witnesses to this transgression of theirs. There was also no one she could call out to for help.

"Look at me," Talia said. "There's nothing to fear. Truly."

Viola forced herself to behold her sister in the water. Talia's form quivered, as if it too were wet and cold like she was, then settled back into a steady state.

Viola bent down and reached out to touch her sister's face. The instant she dipped a finger in the water, Talia crumbled. Pieces of her were shaken and tossed about, a potpourri stirred in a bowl, transforming her into a swirl of colours. Like a watercolour smudged.

Viola drew back her finger promptly, aghast at the swirling jumble her sister had become. After several, long moments that Viola was certain would never come to an end, Talia's form was once more as whole and substantial as before.

"I am only your reflection," Talia said when ripples ceased to crease her face. "I do not exist without you."

The truth about Talia hit Viola like a punch in the gut. "How can that be? You're lying." The leash was still tied to her hands. She threw the other end of it into the water.

"Are you trying to fish me out?" Talia laughed.

"That's what it looks like, doesn't it?"

"You don't need to," Talia said. "Wherever you go, I'm always with you. You don't need a mirror to see me. But where there's a mirror you can peer into, I'll remain trapped in it."

Viola instantly knew what to do. She stepped back from the edge of the lake so she could no longer see herself reflected in its water. Talia reappeared on the shore, arms crossed in front of her chest, her blindfold back on her eyes, even the leash binding her wrist to Viola's, as if she had been standing there on firm land all along.

Viola gaped at her until Talia laughed and said, "Do I have to spell it out to you all over again?"

"It doesn't make any sense."

Viola turned around slowly, feasting on the sights around her. The ground she stood on was a cobblestone path. Beside it was an apple grove. Rows and rows of apple trees stood bearing fruits. Not all were as tall as the one she and Talia had scampered up while Prince Alahaid's men scoured the woods beyond for them.

Facing the grove was the lake. It was so large its waters ran to the horizon. Reflections of clouds floated like boats on its face, perfectly imitating their mates in the sky above.

The cobblestone path unfurled in front of them, dipping and rising, then merged with a muddy trail that ran between the lake and a vast pasture.

A castle in the far distance. Stone walls and steep turrets. Flags fluttering in the breeze. Beckoning.

Talia. Blindfolded. The piece of cloth pressing her ears to her face. Tighter than was necessary. Drawing attention to her full lips and a sharp, determined chin.

Viola ran a finger along her own jawline, trying to conjure up an image of herself. How many hours had she spent caressing Ronin's jaws, drawing the contours of his face in her mind's eye? Without a mirror to look into, something in which to behold her own self, she had hardly felt the need to imagine what she herself looked like.

Her body had been as mysterious as the heart that throbbed within her chest. There had been no call to peer inside and see what her heart really looked like, how it quivered and beat, quickening and slowing in harmony with the rest of her, a coordination that required no intervention from her.

She looked at her hands. Caked with mud and dirt. She looked down at her boots. They were the colour of tree bark. She hitched her skirt and looked at her legs and knees. Could they be deemed shapely?

She looked up at Talia once more. Her hair streaming out from under the blindfold, falling in soft waves over her shoulders and running down to her hips. Viola looked down at her own tresses. Just as long and curly.

Talia. Slender. Reed-like. Willing to bend to her fate. Is that why she had been spared? Salvation by way of surrender?

For Viola could now see what Queen Sahana had intended when she had had every mirror broken, every body of water obscured from view, every shiny metal dulled in the land of Parinara. Her Majesty had banished reflections from her land. Reflections that told you the truth of who you were.

"Where are the others then?" Viola asked. "The other reflections, I mean."

"Severed from their owners. Some hid in the shadows of their masters. But most are trapped where they were last seen. In mirrors that were shattered and crushed. In blades of steel whose shine has been rubbed away. Those can never be retrieved."

"And the Queen's?"

Talia sighed. "She may have very well obliterated hers. That had been her intention after all."

Viola had a sudden urge to rip off the constraint from the eyes of her sister. No. Her reflection.

A strange loneliness engulfed her. For fifteen years she had grown up believing she had a sibling. A mate. A companion. A friend. Two sisters who could see nothing but knew everything. About themselves. About each other.

Only to be told now that one of them wasn't real. Which one?

A soft laugh escaped Viola's lips. A few moments of looking at her reflection had driven her down an endless path of rumination and imaginings. If this is how an encounter with one's own reflection transpired, no wonder Queen Sahana had pursued the only course of action that promised to preserve her sanity.

"What's funny?" Talia asked.

"Nothing. Also, everything."

Talia nodded and gave a little smile. A smile that could be interpreted as understanding. Or condescending. Smug. Little Miss-know-it-all. She had known the truth all along and not breathed a single word.

Anger rose like an unexpected swirl of smoke in Viola. As though sensing it, Talia drifted towards her and touched her arm.

"I couldn't tell you as long as we were in Parinara," Talia said. "But I stayed with you, as much as I could. Others don't even know what they are missing."

Viola looked at Talia, an eyebrow raised in question. Realization dawned upon her. "You were there," she gasped, "the day Ronin challenged me."

"Yes," Talia said, her voice barely a whisper. As if she were afraid her admission would be used against her somehow. "I am always with you. Though I try to be discreet when the situation demands."

A blush of embarrassment coloured Viola's neck and

cheeks. The two of them had been inseparable alright, back when she had believed they were sisters. But to know that Talia had been around, even watched, when Viola had put her arms around Ronin's neck and brought his lips down to meet hers. Something strange and uneasy crawled up Viola's back. She was flabbergasted.

Even more startling was the realisation that Ronin's eyes had widened in horror not at the sight of Viola but when his gaze had settled upon Talia. The spitting image of Viola. Had he known even then who Talia was?

Is that why Talia had dragged Viola right out of Parinara into a strange, unfamiliar world where unknown dangers lurked, ready to spring at them?

"But how?" Viola asked. "I used to discard the leash every time I went to meet Ronin."

Talia slipped the leash over her wrist and dropped it to the ground. Nothing happened. Which is what she had hoped to demonstrate. "The leash is only symbolic," she said. "For my safety. So that I won't be separated from you. Unless you look into a mirror, into a surface that can reflect, unless you have the ability to look outwards, there is no place for me to exist away from you."

Viola began to pace up and down. Confusion, fear and rage gnawed at her insides all at once. "Why didn't you ever tell me?"

"You could have banished me, you know?"

Talia's hand slipped from Viola's arm. Her head hung low between her shoulders. Even blindfolded, she was unable to look at Viola.

"But why would I ever do that?" Viola asked.

"Madness requires no reason, Viola. It is what compelled

Her Majesty to do the unthinkable. Others have lost their reflections without even knowing it. It is one thing to not know what you've lost and quite another to see and choose what you can simply discard. Even siblings do not tolerate each other all the time."

It was strange to receive answers to questions Viola had never thought to ask.

When she was a child, she must have been full of wonder and curiosity. Always demanding to touch and taste, to hear and feel everything in her vicinity. Had she wondered about the blindfold over her eyes?

Or had she taken to it the way she must have accepted the cotton dresses her mother, now long dead, had surely draped her in when the sun was hot or the layers of woollen garments she was cloaked in when the land froze and the cold air chilled her lungs? Had she taken the blindfold to be yet another garment meant to keep her warm and safe? Protect her from the cruelties of the world?

The gift of sight was suddenly too overpowering. Viola put her blindfold back on, higher up so it didn't grate the skin on her cheekbone, skin that had already been rubbed raw and red as blush.

With her sight constrained once more, Viola paid attention to the world around her.

Leaves rustled, whispering secrets to each other. Birds chirped overhead. Larks. Nightingales. Sparrows. The lake was placid in its depths, but a cool breeze rippled its surface, almost soundlessly, but loud enough for Viola to discern. The scent of earth and sweat rose from her body.

When her eyes had been open, she had quickly grown oblivious to the scents and sounds around her.

With eyes shut tight, she sensed the world for what it was, perceived it as it truly was, without colouring it with her visual impressions.

Without the ability to see, she only sought to understand. Not to judge or evaluate.

She breathed in deeply, the rich, fruity scent of tame land a welcome change from the decaying odour of fallen leaves fertilizing the wild forest floor.

The aroma of a meal being cooked somewhere. Stew being stirred in a pot. A song riding on the breeze. A hum.

She felt around with her legs for the leash Talia had dropped to the ground. Finding it, she picked it up and slipped it over her sister's wrist once more.

Yes. Her sister. Or a friend. An imaginary friend, if you will. But a companion, nonetheless. Like a shadow. A part of her, yet quite distinct in her own way. Reliant on external forces to be brought to life.

"You're not me," Viola said. "I am not you. You're an image of me. But who's to say I'm not an image of you too? We may not be one, but that need not prevent us from being together."

Talia gripped Viola's hand in hers. Viola expected to feel different. She looked for the ways in which Talia's revelations might have changed things between them. But there were none.

It was all in her head, Viola realized, how she chose to regard her own reflection.

As an equal partner. Someone who could show her the truth about herself.

Or with indifference. An entity with no standing of its own.

Or with rage. Like Queen Sahana had done. With a refusal

to confront the limitations of who she was and what she could do.

"I'm starving," Talia said. "These apples aren't quite adequate."

Viola couldn't help but laugh. Talia, always the pragmatic one. She too must have caught the fragrance of a home-cooked meal on the breeze.

"That makes two of us," Viola said, and she walked with her sister, hand in hand, towards the first place where they could feed their stomachs and rest their bodies and minds, both sore and tired.

CHAPTER 5

HOME AWAY FROM HOME

They didn't have to walk far. The hum floating on the breeze showed them the way.

It led them to a young woman who was stirring a pot of stew on a cooking fire. The aroma of broth and spices mingled with the sharp, acrid smell of fire and smoke. Viola's mouth watered. The fire warmed their tired limbs.

The woman had an infant strapped to her chest. The baby's gurgles and the mother's coos, even though soft and tender, had been audible to the sisters from miles away.

A soft tinkle occasionally emerged from the woman. Bangles. Or anklets with tiny bells. No, bangles. Certainly. The tinkles were not accompanied by footfall.

The absence of other human sounds was strangely comforting yet unnerving at the same time. Fewer people to explain themselves to. But why was the place deserted?

"Parinaryans?" the woman inquired. Her voice was not accusatory, the way the guard's had been.

"Yes, ma'am," Talia nodded, and Viola could feel her curtsey. She followed suit. For someone who was only a reflection,

26

Talia exhibited way more initiative and wit than anyone else Viola had ever seen.

The young mother laughed. An easy laugh. Guileless. "I'm only a maid. You need not bob to me."

Her child laughed too, a kind of gurgling sound, as if he were joining in the joke. He was more likely delighted at the sound of his mother's laughter.

"I'd bow without thought to anyone who can concoct a stew so delicious it had my belly growling for more than a mile," Talia said. Viola pictured her flashing an easy smile, a charming one.

"Ah! So that's what you two wandering women seek," the woman said with mock admonishment in her voice. And then, more kindly, "I'd have invited you to partake of this meal, nonetheless. No Anansian permits a visitor to pass by unfed." The baby cooed, as if in agreement.

"Thank you," Talia said. "We've been walking for two nights and two days and have only had an apple or two to appease our hunger."

"Please wait here," the woman said. There was a shuffling of feet, the sound of footsteps retreating. A door being pulled open. The soft scraping of thatched straw on mud. The infant's murmurs growing more distant. Footsteps returning. Something being slapped against the ground they stood on.

"Sit," the woman commanded.

Viola and Talia stepped forward gingerly. Mats woven from dry reed had been placed in front of them. They plonked themselves on the mats, overpowered by exhaustion.

Stew splashed into wooden bowls. It was a welcoming sound. The woman placed their bowls in their hands, letting go only when she was certain they had gotten a firm grip on their vessels.

The sisters put their bowls to their lips and guzzled greedily, one spoonful at a time too inadequate to satiate their hunger. Warm, spicy broth coated their throats and sloshed in their bellies, its heat radiated from within them and spread outwards through their limbs to the tips of their fingers and toes. They then felt around in their bowls for the larger chunks of meat or vegetables, scooped them out with their fingers and into their mouths.

Without asking, the woman ladled more stew into their bowls, which disappeared almost as quickly as the first serving had.

It must have been the quietest feast. Only the flames crackled and the baby gurgled, as the hungry sisters slurped and chewed. After a while, even the baby fell silent, likely lulled to sleep by the rhythm of a quiet mealtime.

"What brings you to Anansia?" the woman asked.

Viola hesitated, torn between a desire to unburden herself to their gracious host and the constraint imposed by a lifelong practice of never having interacted with strangers from lands other than Parinara. Everyone was equally limited in sight in Parinara, with their blindfolds on. But they had never spoken with someone who didn't know their ways.

As always, Talia was the one who supplied an answer that was noncommittal but could hardly offend their welcoming host. "We lost our way," she said simply.

If the woman did not believe them, she made no movement or gesture indicating so.

"Anansia is a long way from Parinara," she said quietly. "The woods are filled with unnamed dangers."

Viola's heart froze for an instant. Talia gasped audibly. "How lucky we are then to not have to rely on our eyes to show us the way!"

Talia's deflection worked. The woman didn't ask them any more questions about their improbably journey. Instead, she said, "Have you never wondered what the world looks like? How it truly appears?"

The woman was full of questions. It struck Viola as odd at first. But she told herself their host was merely being curious.

Yet, Viola decided to remain mum and not stand in the way of how Talia chose to answer their host's questions. No one seemed to mind her silence, anyway. Besides, the silent baby, fast asleep now, was probably grateful about Viola's decision to not add to the soft murmurs and whispers Talia and the young maid were engaged in.

Viola felt a tug at her leash, pulling her out of her thoughts.

"I don't need eyes to tell you that you have a beautiful face," Talia was saying. "Oval. A large forehead. A long nose. Full lips. Shapely ears. A long neck."

Talia was running her hands over the woman's face. Conjuring up a mental image of their host. Showing her how much Parinaryans could see without really seeing.

"Your baby takes after you," Talia was now saying. "The same high cheeks and large forehead. Ooh! Look at these precious tiny ears. Like seashells."

Talia then pulled back—the leash slackened—and asked, "Where is everyone else?"

"The village received summons from the King, our Protector and Guardian. His Majesty will soon be on his way to meet the Good Lord, our Maker and Creator. Every able man, woman, and child has gone to the palace to pay their last respects. The baby was unwell this morning, so I stayed behind."

Talia relaxed, not in a way that their host would have noticed, but Viola could sense a lowering of her shoulders, an uncoiling from her belly, and the escape of a breath she had been holding.

Viola had always known what Talia was going through and she had thought it was because they shared a close bond, they were each other's best friend. Viola had taken a certain pride in that, knowing how many other siblings in the village tended to fall out with each other almost every day. But perhaps their closeness had to do with them being each other's reflections, it occurred to her now. The thought confused her. She didn't know what to feel about that. Sad? Or glad?

"Does that make Anansia vulnerable?" Talia asked. "We heard rumours of a war when we entered the kingdom."

"War?!" The woman practically shrieked. Her baby stirred and she shushed and rocked it, lulled it back to sleep. "Is Anansia under attack?"

Talia retreated. "Oh, nothing like that at all. Or perhaps it wasn't in Anansia that we heard the soldiers talk about war. It may have been in another kingdom. Even Borani and Silstila share borders with Anansia and Parinara, you know."

A loud sigh escaped the woman's lips. "I grew up hearing tales of the war that almost raged between Anansia and Parinara. It was the only thing my parents and every one of their generation could ever talk about. It shaped their childhoods, you see. It changed their lives."

"You mean the secret war that almost took place when King Janaheed turned down Queen Sahana's hand in marriage?" The words were out of Viola's mouth before she even knew it. Their host and Talia snapped their heads around to look at Viola, as if only now registering her presence in their midst.

"What do *you* know about that?" Talia and their host asked in unison.

CHAPTER 6

BURDENS OF THE PAST

Talia's question startled Viola out of her reverie. She thought back to what she had said, about the war that Queen Sahana of Parinara had waged against King Janaheed of Anansia.

It was true that this part of the story had been erased from legend. No Parinaryan had been permitted to speak of the way the Queen had thundered down the northern mountains after beheading the Seer who had revealed her true future, one of bitter loneliness.

She had gathered the best of her soldiers, trained with them for several months, and led them stealthily into Anansia.

She had found her way into the chambers of King Janaheed's wife, Queen Renila, in the dead of the night, with every intent of beheading her, only to find an infant in her arms, barely a few days old.

The little one had looked up at her and cooed. Gurgled. As if he were saying *Hello! Who are you? What are you doing here? Have you come to see me? Have you come to play with me?*

Those were the questions that had been raging through

Queen Sahana's head that very instant, questions she was asking her own self.

Who was she? What had she become?

What was she doing there? In the chambers of the Queen of Anansia?

In the room of a mother tending to her infant even as the rest of the world slept around them?

There she stood. Queen Sahana of Parinara.

There she stood. Sword in hand.

Ready to behead another Queen. Ready to rob a newborn of the opportunity to grow up in its mother's embrace?

Disgust filled Queen Sahana's heart. Her sword fell from her hands with a clang that was muffled by the thick rug that cloaked the floor.

Queen Renila approached the intruder, clasped her hand and placed it on the infant's head. "Prince Alahaid," she introduced him. "Bless him, Your Highness."

Queen Sahana had looked into the child's green eyes and seen her own face reflected at her. A face pinched and drawn tight, tense and ravaged from months of plotting and fantasizing about vengeance. A long-ago beauty marred by rage.

This is what King Janaheed saw when he had sauntered into his wife's chambers, wanting to ensure all was well with her and their child, the dutiful husband that he was.

He saw a mad woman dressed for war, anger and confusion in her golden eyes, angry brown stripes painted on her cheeks, her sword by her feet, her hand on his child's head.

With a roar and two strides he was upon her. He dragged her away from his wife and child and pushed her to the ground.

He pinned her arms behind her back, paying no heed to

the fact that she offered no resistance, paying no heed to the explanations his soft-spoken wife was sending his way, paying no heed to his startled child who had now begun to wail.

He called out to the guards and commanded them to throw the intruder into prison.

Only when she allowed herself to be dragged away, limp as a bag of dead stones, did he pick up the sword and notice the seal of Parinara on its pommel. A hawk with its wings spread out, poised for flight.

King Janaheed turned to his wife and their child and held them in his embrace until her shoulders no longer trembled and the baby no longer wailed, until the shock had worn off from their startled faces and their tense bodies.

Then he had marched out of their room and down to the prison where the intruder he now recognized as Queen Sahana was being held captive.

"Forgive me," she had whispered from behind the bars of her cell, cowering like a shadow in the darkest corner so he wouldn't see her shame or guilt.

Queen Sahana of Parinara. A haughty and proud princess, once upon a time. Now, a lost soul. Pitiful.

The kind King of Anansia had ordered the distraught Queen of Parinara to be released, after having extracted a promise from her that she'd never set eyes on anything good and pure with the intention of destroying it, that no Parinaryan shall ever bring harm to an Anansian.

In a fit of repentance, Queen Sahana had returned to Parinara and transformed it into a land of no eyes, a land of no reflections.

A land whose truth disappeared like mist being dispelled

by sunlight, and all that remained was a legend long forgotten and never spoken of.

"I'VE NEVER HEARD that story before," Talia said.

"You couldn't possibly have heard it," the young woman said. "Only Anansians know about the almost-war with Parinara. It is not a secret we willingly share with anyone outside our kingdom. Kindness can be misconstrued as weakness."

"Someone must have revealed the secret," Talia said. "Viola, who told you this story?"

Their tones sounded accusatory to Viola, or she may have imagined it, for in that instant she felt guilty of possessing this nugget of knowledge even though she couldn't, for the life of her, explain how she had come to own it.

"I can't explain," she said simply. "I didn't know I knew this truth."

She felt Talia's hand on her arm. A firm touch. A reassuring one. Then, turning to their host, Talia said, "It must have been terrible for the older generation of Anansia to have lived like that. Under constant threat of danger."

"Her Majesty, Queen Renila, was never the same again," the woman said. "She lived in endless fear for the rest of her days. Not fear for her own life, but for her son's. They could have been killed on a moment's whim."

She fell quiet. Her fear was palpable. That a child could have been lost so easily, that too the Crown Prince himself, was enough to strike terror in the heart of any new mother.

The young woman feeding two wanderers from Parinara

was no exception to the affliction of constant anxiety that bringing up a child imposed on parents.

"Sometimes my mother would lament that they could have moved on had there truly been a war," she continued. "Even when Parinara became a land of no eyes, a land of no reflection, Anansia couldn't quite shake off the terror that your queen's trespasses had inflicted in the hearts of our people. Living in constant fear ate away at their souls."

There it was. In the way their host referred to the Queen of Parinara. Not as Queen Sahana. But as 'your Queen'.

By changing a mere word, she had drawn a line between herself and the two sisters, between the Anansians and the Parinaryans under her roof. Danger hung like a grey cloud over the sisters, threatening to explode into torrential rain any moment now.

Talia rose. Feeling the tug on her leash, Viola stood up too. "You have been very kind to us," Talia said to the woman. "We cannot thank you enough for feeding us. We must be on our way now."

"Where will you go?"

"To pay homage to King Janaheed," Talia declared, much to Viola's surprise. "I believe his men are looking for us."

CHAPTER 7

AN ACT OF SURRENDER

"What are we doing?" Viola hissed to Talia as they rode towards the castle on Kinara, a black stallion lent to them by their host.

"How long do you think it will take them to find us? Two blind girls that we are?" Talia scoffed. "This way we may not be beheaded at sight. A voluntary surrender may keep us alive for a little longer."

Viola shivered. Daylight still lit up the world around them. She could sense the light beyond her blindfold. Layers of light like shimmering waves and swirls. Constantly moving. Shape-shifting.

It was different at night. Just an endless darkness, thick and deep. The sounds at night were different too. More hushed. More stealthy. The silence could be so thick that the slightest of sounds was easily discerned. A fox's snuffle could sound loud and clear, piercing the sky like a sword through its heart.

But now there was a different sound altogether. A low rumbling in the distance. Not the noiseless gathering of clouds on the horizon ahead of a thunderstorm. But a jumble of sounds. Hooves kicking dirt. Boots on rocks. Whispers. Conversations. Yelps. Wails. Laughter. Snorts.

It came towards them, rising in volume and intensity. Human voices. Throngs of them.

Then it swarmed around them like bees surrounding a hive. A stream parting to flow around a tall boulder. Not quite. Because it still maintained a respectable distance from the riders. Their stallion, Kinara, was not perturbed. He continued at his pace. Steady. But not rushed.

The girls strained their ears to catch snippets of conversations even though the people passing them by stayed away from them.

Talia shot an arm up towards the sky, dragging Viola's along. "Greetings, Anansians!"

At the sound of her voice, the murmurs faded. Talia waited until the silence was absolute, and then she said, "We are on our way to pay our respects to His Highness, King Janaheed."

More silence. Kinara continued to trot slowly. Without her feet on firm ground, Viola felt uncertain. The stirrups swayed and barely conveyed the impression of stability. But Talia felt more powerful up here, addressing the crowd from a pedestal of sorts rather than getting down at eye level with them.

"King Janaheed is dead! King Alahaid is now the ruler of Anansia." It was a young child's voice. Sweet and honest. Truthful.

The murmur of voices rose once more like an ocean wave, foaming and frothing, making its way, poised to curl and topple over itself onto the shore, threatening to drag and drown the sisters as it collapsed.

"Please accept our condolences, Anansians," Talia said,

pulling her hand back down. She placed it over her chest. "My sister and I have forever lost the good fortune of paying homage to the kind king who spared our parents' land long before we were even born."

Viola's heart pounded in her chest. She couldn't tell how many Anansians were walking past them, but she found a little solace in the fact that Kinara hadn't stopped. No one had approached too close to their horse. Not yet at least.

Viola couldn't wait to move past them and leave them far behind enough that they wouldn't pose any danger. She couldn't shirk the feeling that something was amiss, something in Talia's words had been inappropriate and should not have been uttered in the first place.

"*You* are not supposed to know that," someone yelled. A man's voice. From behind. Far behind them.

Talia pulled the horse's reins and brought it to a halt. *Wrong move*, Viola wanted to whisper in Talia's ears, but the silence that had fallen around them was so still and thick she was afraid of perturbing it and drawing unwanted attention to her words. She kept mum.

"Only an Anansian by birth knows the true saga. Only a true Anansian can tell myth apart from the truth."

Talia inhaled, then let out a deep sigh. She turned Kinara around until she faced the speaker. "You are right, Sir," she said, her voice dripping with humility. "We learnt the truth only this morning, when the sun wasn't as high in the sky as it is now. We learnt the truth only after setting foot in your welcoming land."

"Who welcomed you here?" The voice was closer now. Still far enough to not prompt the young women into turning around and galloping away.

"A new mother who gave us food and warmth and kindness the way she does for her infant," Talia replied. Her spine was erect, her shoulders straight, her chest out, but her chin tucked in. She wanted to display confidence and courage, not arrogance and affront.

But Viola was crouched behind Talia, in as much of a foetal position as she could manage astride a horse. She curled into herself. Her legs almost squeezed Kinara although she tried not to, knowing it might prompt the horse into a gallop. Her arms were wrapped around her chest, and she hunched low, as if hiding behind Talia's back.

"Halt!" a familiar voice shouted. It came from a distance, from the direction they were facing.

A deafening sound of hooves on the ground. Horses galloping. Their riders urging them to go faster. A cloud of dust settled upon the sisters. Mud and sand cloaked them like second skin and brought on a coughing fit.

"Seize them!" the voice commanded. It was the voice of the captain who had instructed his little gathering of soldiers to scour the woods for the culprits who had rendered their comrade unconscious.

"What is our crime, Sir?" Talia asked. Viola held herself tighter to keep from trembling. Even though the sun was high in the sky and poured pleasant warmth over Anansia, Viola's body was seized with chills and her teeth chattered.

The leader snorted. "I must correct you, young lady. Crimes. Not crime. Trespassing on Anansia. Deceit. Lying about your true identity. Attacking a soldier of Anansia. All these are crimes serious enough for you two to be executed, were you not too young to have your lives snatched away from you."

Thank Heavens for small mercies, Viola thought with a shudder.

But then the captain said, "A few years in the dungeons is perhaps a more fitting punishment. That ought to teach you a lesson. But our benevolent Prince has ordained that you will be returned to your land, that you will face the penalty your ruler deems fit."

"Please forgive us our trespasses, Sir," Talia said. She sounded unfazed, not at all betraying the fact that returning to Parinara was akin to a fate worse than death. By now Queen Sahana must have gotten wind of what Viola had done, how she had pulled off her blindfold and opened her eyes to look at Ronin. If Viola were to return to Parinara, she'd be marched straight to the guillotine.

"A woman should not be punished for her attempts to keep herself safe," Talia said. "Surely the honourable King Alahaid would see merit in our rationale."

There was a shuffling of feet and a low murmur. Words were spoken, and the sisters could discern what was being said. A member of the crowd returning from the palace informed the captain of the demise of King Janaheed. The soldiers had been looking for Talia and Viola all morning. News of their king's demise hadn't yet reached their ears.

Of course, Talia must have known this very obvious fact and had sought to unsettle the captain by delivering to him the news of his king's demise. Viola could only hope Talia's words would have the intended effect. What if the captain flew at them in a fit of rage and grief and beheaded them then and there?

But when the captain spoke again, it was with a gravity

that gave away his grief. "Chain them and bring them to the palace," he said to his comrades. Viola dared to exhale.

A soldier rode up to Kinara and slipped cuffs on the sisters' hands. He permitted Talia to hold on to the horses' reins however, a fact that gave Viola some solace because she was now worried that unable to hold on to anything, they'd fall off the horse and meet their maker under Kinara's hooves. The soldier then turned Kinara around, roped him to his own horse, and led the girls to the palace.

CHAPTER 8

WORTHY OF SIGHT?

It was at times like these that Viola wished she could enjoy the gift of sight. The soldier who led their horse spoke with the girls occasionally, mostly prompted by Talia's inquiries about him and his life in Anansia.

He described to them how the king's castle was made of white marble and grey stone, how a dozen turrets kept it safe, how it appeared welcoming and formidable at the same time, inviting friends, warning foes away, how the flags were flying at half-mast to announce the demise of their king, how King Janaheed had been a just ruler and that Prince Alahaid, now King Alahaid, was certain to carry on his father's good reputation.

Talia made her queries sound innocuous. Like harmless gossip, encouraging the soldier who insisted she call him by his name. Inniyeth. But nothing about Talia was innocuous, Viola knew. She was gathering information.

Poor Prince—no, King—Alahaid, now an orphan, both his parents gone.

Oh, is he not betrothed to anyone?

How many children do you have, Inniyeth? Oh, you're not married? A kind man such as yourself, not spoken for yet?

What types of crops are cultivated in Anansia?

What a pleasant day!

The soldier pointed out to her that the skies were a clear, cloudless blue, to which Talia put her hand on her heart and said, "In our land, it is a blessing to die under a clear sky. The soul then has an unobstructed path to the Heavens. It means that God is waiting to welcome your soul to His abode."

Viola rolled her eyes inside her blindfold. Talia was concocting the most ridiculous of stories.

In the past three decades, no one in Parinara had been able to tell whether the sky was clear or cloudy. Unless it rained or snowed, unless thunder growled and lightning cracked, unless a cloud blotted out the face of the sun only to peel itself away after a while, it was quite difficult to conjure up an image of the sky in their heads.

No matter how sharp their other senses had become, the loss of sight was one that Parinaryans could never completely compensate for.

Some things in this world were meant to be seen and beheld. Their beauty could be perceived only by sight.

The wild colours of a sunset. The blinding light of the sun.

The resplendent sheen of a full, bulbous moon. The dance of sunlight and leaf-shadow in summer.

The twirl of snowflakes in winter. The contours of snow-capped mountain peaks against the sky at dawn.

No amount of poetry or sculpture could ever reproduce the beauty of the original. There was always something lacking in description.

Viola found herself drifting away, tuning out the conversation Talia was keeping up with Inniyeth. She wondered what kind of lives people lived when their reflections did not accompany them like a superior sibling but existed merely to imitate them, do as they were told, instead of exhibiting initiative.

A life without Talia. What would that be like?

The thought first sent Viola down a path of guilt, remorse for wishing her sister, her reflection, away. It was like wanting to do away with a part of herself. That kind of desire came with its own special brand of self-loathing.

But once she transcended that feeling of remorse, there came a sense of possibility. More curiosity than repentance plagued her.

She could ask herself once more. What would a life without Talia truly be like? As strange as it might feel at first, Viola would most likely get accustomed to being by herself, living life by herself, without Talia to show the way.

The more she thought about it, imagining herself seated at the front, holding the reins of Kinara, carrying on a casual conversation with a stranger who was now pouring out his heart's secrets to a blindfolded young woman even though she was likely less than a day away from being executed, the more exhilarating all the possibilities seemed.

Then an equally shocking thought entered her head. What if Talia too had been plotting a way to rid herself of Viola? Fear formed a knotty lump at the base of Viola's throat and pressed hard upon her chest.

But no. That wasn't possible, was it? Talia had revealed, in no uncertain terms, that she wouldn't exist without Viola. It was Viola who had the power to banish Talia, not the other way round.

Recalling Talia's words about how she never wanted to be separated mollified Viola somewhat. But if she, Viola, was truly the more powerful of the two, why did it feel as if she was walking in her reflection's shadow?

Talia had ruled their lives for as long as she could remember. They had become orphans at a very young age, so young that Viola had very few memories of her mother and father.

They grew up in a distant aunt's home that was filled with so many grown-ups and children it was impossible to distinguish who was related to whom by birth.

Besides, by the time her extended family had taken Viola into their fold, everyone had already been living blindfolded for more than two decades. Relationships and possessions had tended to become more communal than individual in nature. Along with sight, discernment and preferences were eroded too.

Such an arrangement meant that Viola and Talia could slip away unnoticed, skip off to their own adventures, as long as they returned in time for meals and dutifully completed the chores they were assigned. Nobody missed them or paid any heed to them otherwise. Talia's unusual presence went entirely unnoticed.

Without the rest of the world to direct their attention towards, most of the older Parinaryans, especially those who had enjoyed the privilege of sight before the Queen's disastrous mandate, fell into the unfortunate trend of doing as little as they could, laying blame on their lack of sight for their reluctance to live more fully, more wholeheartedly.

Talia had been the only constant in her life. Viola had never found reason to evaluate Talia's instinctive ability to lead. She had never sought to question Talia's motives.

But knowing that Talia's very existence depended on her caused Viola to wonder. Had Talia truly been the soul sister Viola had always believed her to be? Or had it all just been a sham, a charade constructed by Talia with the sole objective of preserving her existence?

It all made sense now, in hindsight. Talia had been sly enough to not draw the attention of anyone who'd realize how wrong her presence was, how impossible her very existence was in a land that held no place for reflections. She had always been careful to not draw attention to her true self. At the same time, she had established herself so firmly in Viola's life that the latter had never had reason to believe something was amiss.

Yet, whatever her reasons may have been, Talia was the one who had dragged Viola out of Parinara after that misadventure with Ronin. Talia had saved Viola from having to face Queen Sahana's wrath even though with every trot, Kinara was leading them closer and closer to that very fate they had sought to escape.

Viola herself probably had less than a day to live, which meant Talia would be wiped out too. It was a sobering eventuality, and Viola chided herself for the uncharitable thoughts she had been harbouring towards her sister in these past few moments.

She resolved to do better. She'd much rather spend these precious moments delighting in the antics of her lifelong companion, for no matter who Talia was or what she may have done, life with her had been immensely entertaining. There had never been a dull moment.

"You should come visit us someday," Talia was saying to

Inniyeth when Viola drew her attention back to their conversation. She couldn't believe her ears.

Neither could Inniyeth for he snorted and said, "An Anansian in Parinara? Forgive me for saying this but I have no wish to be blindfolded."

"Ah, yes! I can see how that can be a severe detriment," Talia replied, ever the unabashed one. Never one to be thrown off by rejection.

"But—," Inniyeth began, then paused, taking a moment to deliberate whether or not it was wise for him to utter the words he had been about to say.

"Go on," Talia coaxed.

"If all goes as planned, we might find ourselves making our way to Parinara tomorrow," he said quietly.

All that he left unsaid hung in the air between them. Like a threat. Because if all went as planned, King Alahaid and his soldiers would head to Parinara to hand Talia and Viola over to Queen Sahana.

Even Talia couldn't completely shrug off the gloom that Inniyeth's words cast upon them. They rode the rest of the way in silence.

Neither consumed by thoughts nor distracted by Talia's attempts at charming any living being in her vicinity, Viola listened to the sounds around her.

Bells pealed in the distance. The delicate fragrance of roses and the thickly sweet scent of raisins and nuts wafted her way. Likely a temple. A place of worship.

Hustle and bustle. Vendors displaying and advertising their wares, calling out to passersby. Negotiations. Shouts to buy cloth of the blackest silk for the King's funeral. A marketplace. Viola and Talia heard the sounds long before they approached the market centre of Anansia.

"Your king has died, and vendors continue to sell their wares?" Talia asked.

"These men and women need their day's earnings to feed themselves and their families," Inniyeth explained. He had a soothing, patient voice, the kind one used to read bedtime stories to children. "Our late king, may his soul rest in peace, would have been aghast had any of his actions, whether in life or in death, deprived these poorest of the poor of their daily meals."

"Why would the king not just give them a daily wage, a minimum, something to at least ensure they wouldn't starve even as they go about their daily work?"

"I wondered, too, when I was old enough to think about such matters."

"Great minds!" Talia said with a giggle. "We think alike."

"Fools do too!" Inniyeth said with much mirth in his voice. "But I've since learnt that nothing given away freely is ever valued. Our people take much pride in their work. To take that away from them would be sanctimonious."

For a moment, Viola couldn't tell if Inniyeth was being serious or not. He sounded sincere, but his argument was without merit, as far as she was concerned. The rich always found ways to justify the struggles of the poor, to explain why they wouldn't do more to help when they so easily could.

There was only one reason for it, Viola had always known. The fewer people possessed wealth, the more valuable it was. Talia too had nothing to say in reply and Viola suspected she felt the same way.

The sounds of life ahead of them were strangely soothing.

But as they approached the marketplace, silence surrounded them wherever they went.

Viola imagined vendors and clients pausing in their conversations to stare at the two blindfolded women on horseback being led by the soldiers of their kingdom. She imagined the questions that must be racing through their minds, the gossip that would spread as soon as the soldiers were out of earshot.

Viola could still catch a few snippets of the hushed whispers and murmurs that resumed in their wake, but the Anansians going about their daily lives in the marketplace on the morning of the demise of King Janaheed would hardly know that.

Sure enough, she heard quiet mumbles of "Parinaryans?"

"What are they doing here?"

"Why are the guards taking them to the palace?"

"Have they heard of King Janaheed's passing?"

"Will Queen Sahana attack Anansia now that our old king has passed away?"

"Prince Alahaid has proven himself more than capable of ruling our kingdom. He will protect us."

For all the fear that had held Viola in its grip, she realized that she too was capable of striking terror in the hearts of many.

She could either look at their strangeness, their unfamiliarity as a curse, a scourge that roused suspicion and disgust in others. Or she could consider it as a tool of power, one that kept people away out of fear.

But people became unpredictable when they were afraid. In the grip of fear, they'd want nothing more than to eradicate the very source of the terror itself.

She sent a silent prayer of thanks skywards for the protection she received as a captive. She and Talia were meant to be taken to the palace and she was certain that no harm would befall them until then.

When they dismounted, it took a while to get used to walking on firm ground again. Her body continued to sway as if she were still astride Kinara, being bobbed about. She stumbled up the steps—there were so many, and she was too tired to count—even though one of the guards had offered his arm for her to hold on to. She didn't need to, but she appreciated his offer of aid. He walked beside her, nonetheless.

No one outside of Parinara knew how, even blindfolded, Parinaryans could navigate unfamiliar places just as fast and adeptly as anybody with the gift of sight. Faster even, without all the distraction others' eyes tended to seek. Talia must have been clutching Inniyeth's arm, Viola was certain.

The guards came to a halt. A swish. Then a mighty heave and a groan. The sound of a pair of heavy gates being swung open by two guards, their boots striking the ground in unison, a rhythm that sounded pleasing to the ears.

The guard beside Viola whispered they were entering the palace grounds. But even without his declaration, even without the steep steps they had navigated to arrive at the gates, Viola had been able to discern where the marketplace had ended and where the royal land had begun.

Rough, rocky terrain gave way to smooth, slippery flagstones. The thick scent of spices and sweat, of attar and fabric that had wrapped around them in the marketplace had dissipated.

Now the air smelled clean and pure, rich with life, a whiff of roses and jasmines and flowers whose fragrances were foreign to her. But the air was also sterile, controlled, the way Viola recognized well-tended gardens smelt, unlike the wild, rich, unpredictable fragrance of untamed woods.

Birds sang sweetly overhead. Light alternately brightened and dimmed so quickly that she realized they were walking in the shade of trees. The dance of leaf-shadow and sunlight was disorienting when she couldn't see it but could only perceive and visualize it in the eye of her mind. Her head throbbed with a dull ache.

On and on they walked in a straight line. The grounds were larger than the marketplace they had crossed.

Up flights of stairs, turning this way and that. When the floor changed from the hardness of flagstone to the lush softness of carpets and rugs, it became evident they were getting closer to their destination. Viola held on to the leash that tied her to Talia, taking comfort in the fact that they were still bound together.

Then came an unexpected shove. Viola fell to the carpet, colliding into Talia who had undoubtedly met a similar fate.

"Don't let them remove our blindfolds," Talia hissed into Viola's ears before she was roughly pulled back to her feet.

"What?" Viola asked, not quite grasping the fact that Talia had uttered a word to her after having completely ignored her in favour of Inniyeth throughout their journey astride Kinara for the past several hours.

But Talia did not have another opportunity to explain or repeat her words, for the captain's voice boomed loud and clear from right behind them.

"Your Majesty, the trespassers from Parinara," the captain of the little troop that had led Viola and Talia to the palace announced.

There was a murmur of apology as Inniyeth helped Talia to her feet and walked away with the others.

Viola and Talia stood. While Viola was not entirely sure where His Majesty, King Alahaid, was seated, Talia remained still. Taking in the King's court where they had been dragged to, but there was hardly any sound to guide her.

A flutter of wings. Talia snapped her head up, from where the sound had originated. Briefly.

A guttural coo. A dove.

"Even a dozen tall men standing one on another's shoulders cannot graze the skylight, Your Majesty," Talia said in awe.

A sudden movement. The sound of boots and the chink of armour. Aborted, just as abruptly.

Two guards had dashed towards Talia to silence her, for how dare she speak before she was spoken to, but the king had gestured them to leave her be. Viola knew of no land in which it was permissible for an ordinary citizen to address royalty before they were spoken to. She trembled, fearful that Talia's insolence would finally cost them their lives.

"And you can discern this by the mere flutter of a bird's wings?"

Both Viola and Talia turned a little towards their right and faced the king directly.

"Yes, Your Majesty," Talia said, bowing low. Viola did as her sister did.

"Very impressive," King Alahaid said. He spoke decisively, without any inflection. His voice was that of one who was to not be disobeyed, not because it was commanding, not at all, but because it was accommodating. As if the king's orders in the land of Anansia were one you followed not because the king had issued them but because you wanted to please him, do what he deemed right. King Alahaid commanded trust. Just as surely as Queen Sahana had become the very epitome of distrust and tyranny.

"Thank you, Your Majesty," Talia said and added, after a breath-long pause. "We offer you our condolences on this day."

King Alahaid said nothing, but the brief swish of his royal robes indicated movement on his part. He had likely shifted in his throne or made a gesture with the briefest flick of a wrist.

"What brings you to Anansia?" he finally asked.

This was no time to lie, Viola wanted to hiss at Talia. It was one thing to lie to a commoner but quite another to conceal the truth from a ruler of the land. A ruler who had the power to determine their fate.

"We were, still are, on the run from the soldiers of Parinara," Talia said, with more than a hint of pride in her voice. "They chased us through the forest. We ran for two nights and two days with no specific destination in mind. It is our good fortune that has brought us to Anansia."

Viola braced herself for the question that was to come. And it did. "And what reason might you two have to be pursued by the soldiers of your land?" King Alahaid asked.

Before Talia could concoct a suitable response, Viola dipped into a bow and said, "It was my fault, Your Majesty. For a dare, I untied my blindfold and opened my eyes."

King Alahaid said nothing in response. Viola felt the slightest tug on her leash, but she couldn't decipher if Talia was gesturing to her to continue speaking or admonishing her for having butted in.

"It is a crime punishable by death in Parinara," King Alahaid said.

"Yes, Your Majesty." Even though the king had not posed a question, Viola had felt the need to emphasize her awareness of the peril she had plunged herself and Talia into. She did not want to be taken for someone who was in the habit of committing brazen misdeeds and expecting to get away with them.

"Anansia is a welcoming land," the King said after a period of silence that seemed interminable. "But your continued presence here could invite the wrath of Queen Sahana, and I will not, under any circumstance, put my people in peril. You two shall spend the night in the palace. We will leave for Parinara at the first light of dawn. I will urge your Queen to exhibit clemency."

Just as Viola thought the King had finished saying all that he wanted to, he added, "Whoever you opened your blindfold for, I hope the person was worthy of your sight."

CHAPTER 9

ENTANGLEMENTS OF THE HEART

The King's parting words rang in Viola's ears as the guards—four in all, she could tell from the loud sound of their resounding march—led them out of the court, once again through long corridors that smelled of musk and autumn, up flights of stairs that curved so gently Viola would have sworn they were walking in a straight line had she not trained herself to discern the slightest bend in the path she was on.

Inniyeth was not among them. Talia kept mum throughout.

King Alahaid was extremely perceptive. Not only had he deduced that Viola must have opened her blindfold to set her greedy eyes on a person of desire, not on an object or even upon her own self, he must have also noticed the growing camaraderie between one of his guards and an intruder from a neighbouring kingdom with which Anansia sought to share only a border and nothing else.

Viola couldn't tell if Inniyeth was worthy of such a transgression but, it occurred to her as they walked on richly carpeted floors under impossibly high ceilings in the palace of the King of Anansia, that sometimes it only took a few moments to truly know and understand someone, but quite often you could know someone for a lifetime and still not perceive the truth about them.

Both Talia and Ronin had become strangers in a single moment of vision. The ones she had known and loved with eyes blindfolded were not the same people she saw with clear eyes, her view unobstructed by layers of folded cloth designed to keep light and the rest of the world forever out of view.

"Come in, please." A woman's gentle voice startled Viola out of her reverie. The marching stomp of the guard's boots already sounded distant. "You are guests of Anansia. I am Noyoni. My sisters and I will attend to every need of yours. We are aware of the astute powers of observation of Parinaryans. But please allow me to show you one important thing."

She clasped Viola's and Talia's hands and led them into what Viola assumed was a room. Gone was the musky scent of the corridors. Here, a garden was in full bloom. Soft roses and jasmines. Understated floral notes. A whiff of lemongrass. It was a woman's chamber.

Noyoni lifted their hands and placed them on a thick coil of rope that hung from the ceiling and ended in a knot in mid-air. "We have been instructed to lock the only door to the room, but you can send for us anytime by tugging on the bell."

Curious, Viola pulled the rope. Birdsong rang in the distance, its melody sweet and unexpected like a faraway spring coaxed to reappear in a land ravaged by drought.

Yet, Anansia was hardly a land ravaged by drought. It was a

land of prosperity and peace. Ruled by a just king, its people were warm and welcoming.

But Anansia was not, could never be, her home, Viola realized. She wanted to commit to memory the soft voice of Noyoni, her words slow and soothing like a lullaby. She wanted to hold on to the melody that lay hidden at the other end of the bell pull, connected to her hand by a thick coil of rope, somehow both sturdy and soft to the touch at the same time.

It was Viola who felt ravaged by drought. In a land so rich and fine, her sightlessness was a blight. The fate that awaited her in Parinara was made worse by the kindness that the people of Anansia showered on her so easily.

Viola and Talia had come here as fugitives. Now they were being treated as royal guests. Tears rolled down her cheeks as she let go of the bell pull, thanked Noyoni, and turned away from her to explore the rest of the chamber.

Talia had already slipped the leash off her hand and was humming a tune. This is how they explored a new area. By producing sound and paying keen attention to how it reflected and bent upon bouncing off the walls and furniture.

Viola did not follow suit. Talia's song and its echoes provided her with adequate information on how large the room was (thrice as large as their home back in Parinara had been), and where the bed was (in the centre, the headrest up against a wall, a four-poster beauty made of ancient wood from what she could decipher). Talia's song bounced off what Viola deduced were little cabinets and dressers on either side of the bed.

Comfortable with her knowledge of the new area, Viola

chose to run her fingers up and down the walls. Embossed motifs of a whole new world came to life upon her touch.

Here was a bird with a crest, like a cardinal, but also a tail longer than the rest of its body. Here was a fruit, partially peeled, which appeared like a flower, but she could tell it was a fruit from the seeds cleverly hidden in its core.

Countless apple trees. A grove. Beside it, a large lake. The ripples on its surface rose to meet Viola's skin as her fingers brushed over them. A trail clinging to one edge of the lake, disappearing into a pasture. Huts. Several in little clusters. Cooking fires right outside them.

In her mind, Viola pulled up the image of the woman and her infant who had fed two strange Parinaryans without fear or disapproval, because that is what Anansians did, welcomed every visitor, whether tourist or vagabond, into their land, into their homes, into their very hearts.

All of Anansia was here on this wall under her fingertips. The castle she and Talia were now housed in. Its stone walls and narrow turrets. The flags of Anansia fluttering, at half-mast, Viola was surprised to find. A living, breathing portrayal of the land she was in.

"No windows." Talia's voice had a sense of urgency to it that startled Viola, and it took her a moment to register the import of her reflection's words.

"What?"

"There are no windows in this room. This place comes with all the bells and whistles only to detract us from the fact that it is nothing but a prison cell in disguise."

Viola shrugged. "It is still better than a prison cell. After the two sleepless nights we've had, I'd much rather sleep in this bed than on a cold floor."

A knock on the door prevented Talia from responding. "Come in," she said.

Noyoni entered with two others. "Dinner is served, my ladies," she announced.

"Thank you," Viola said with a smile. The last meal they had had was the stew that the young mother near the apple orchards had served them. But that had been half a day ago, and Viola was ready and willing to devour a feast meant to feed ten soldiers.

Viola and Talia waited in silence as Noyoni and, presumably, her sisters, placed bowls of delicacies on a large table set against the wall between the door and the bed.

They served various dishes on two plates. Steaming heaps of rice. A stew with the freshest vegetables of the season. Roasted meat. The sticky sweet scent of dessert. Fruit custard, Viola guessed. Her mouth watered, and she could barely wait until Noyoni and her sisters had finished laying the table and backed out, taking their time, reminding the sisters to beckon them for assistance without any hesitation at all.

As soon as the door closed, Viola rushed to the table. She grabbed the fork and knife placed beside her plate, poked her way around the food on her plate for a moment, and began to tuck in.

"Did you hear the lock click?" Talia asked. Her voice did not come from beside Viola but from the far end of the room on the other side of the bed.

"Why aren't you eating?" Viola's words came out minced and muffled as she spoke through a full mouth. The warm mixture of rice and vegetable stew slid down her throat and into her belly, soothing her insides. There was something to be said about the partaking of delicious food at the end of a long, harrowing journey fraught with uncertainties.

Viola had the strange realization that in this moment she felt immensely content. She was so satisfied that even the inevitable prospect of being beheaded by Parinara's executioner the next day could not dampen her spirits in this instant.

"They've locked us in here." Talia said.

Her continued talk of gloom was beginning to wear Viola down. "Of course, they have," she muttered. "We're only prisoners after all. Not royal guests. Which is why you should come here and eat this scrumptious food before the king realises his folly and has us dragged to the dungeons for the rest of the night."

Talia did not move. "What if the food is poisoned?"

Viola paused, but only for a moment. She had pierced a fork into a piece of roasted meat, which she now held in mid-air, right in front of her open mouth. She promptly put it into her mouth and took her time chewing and relishing its juicy flavours, refusing to contaminate this moment of pure joy with imaginary worries of the future.

"Well, what if it is?" Viola said. "I've already scooped three morsels of it into my mouth. If it is indeed laced with poison, it is already corroding my insides, slowly, even as I sit here conversing with you about the relative merits and demerits of finding ourselves in a lavishly furnished and decorated room in the kingdom of Anansia, whose people have been nothing short of kind and welcoming towards us even though the queen of our land once attempted to kill their present ruler. And even if we do not meet our Maker here, tonight, we will encounter Him tomorrow when Queen Sahana instructs her executioner to behead us. And even if we somehow evade that fate, death will catch up to us eventually. So, stop fretting and come here. Sit by my side and eat. It is impossible to think clearly on an empty stomach. And then tell me why you've suddenly turned so paranoid?"

Buoyed by her own monologue, Viola returned to her plate and continued to partake of her meal, relishing each bite, allowing herself to feel the sensation of each flavour and spice bursting on her tongue, before swallowing each morsel, grateful for its satisfying nourishment. She couldn't recall the last time she had enjoyed a meal so much.

"Are you not afraid of dying?" Talia's voice was a whisper, scared and wobbly. She sounded like a small child, terrified.

The question struck Viola as odd. For someone who had shown so much bravado until now, it hadn't occurred to her that Talia could be afraid of death. "Are you?" she asked.

Talia sniffled. She was weeping. Viola got up from the table and went around the bed to where Talia stood, now sobbing loudly, no longer attempting to hide her distress now that Viola had discerned it. Her shoulders shook violently, overpowered by grief. Viola opened her arms wide, and Talia collapsed into them, unable to stand on her own momentarily. Viola led her to the bed and they both sat on its edge, Talia leaning into Viola, as if she no longer wanted to exist outside of her.

Something had changed, Viola realized. Something that had transformed Talia's courage into sheer terror.

Talia. A reflection who had survived unscathed in a land of no reflection for fifteen years. Like a lily in a desert. Or a daffodil. Or a flower the colour of sand in a desert. For she had been well camouflaged.

In a land where no one was permitted to see, it hadn't occurred to anyone that Talia was an oddity. Not one among them. Nothing at all like them, truth be told.

She had managed to survive in that land without rousing any suspicion as to her origins, as to who she truly was. Even Viola hadn't known that Talia was a part of her in a far more familiar way than a sibling could ever be. A part of her that ought to have been banished along with everyone else's in the kingdom.

Viola realized how inane her question to Talia had been. Of course, Talia was petrified of returning to Parinara. Now that Ronin had seen her for who she was, Talia would be punished for having dared to exist. And Viola was certain to be punished for her complicity in Talia's survival. And no, ignorance was not an excuse that would be brooked.

But they had known all of this the instant the captain of the guards of Anansia had stood under the apple tree and commanded his team to scour the woods for the two Parinaryans.

Talia's demeanour had begun to change only after they had left the court of King Alahaid and had been escorted to this room. She had kept up a happy banter until then, conversing easily with the young mother and her infant, addressing a large crowd of curious Anansians while seated upon Kinara, and chatting with Inniyeth all the way to the palace.

Realization struck Viola like light glinting off a piece of glass. "Inniyeth?" she whispered.

Talia's sobs grew louder.

Whoever said the truth shall set you free had certainly failed to mention all the havoc it first tended to wreak before lighting a path to freedom.

"Oh, you poor thing!" Viola hugged Talia tighter and ran her fingers through her hair.

It wasn't the most natural of tasks because Talia's blindfold came in the way like a bump interrupting the smooth flow of Viola's fingers. A constant reminder of why Talia couldn't have a life of her own, couldn't fall in love with another and hope to have a lifelong companion of her own. She was merely a reflection. Dragged along wherever Viola went.

Even a shadow fared better than a reflection did. A shadow could survive under the dimmest of starlight. The rightful place of a reflection was on the other side a mirror.

Yet, in the land where all mirrors had been destroyed, Talia had somehow survived and now she could exist as herself, on her own, only where there were no surfaces for reflection. No boundaries that could separate a person from their mirror image. Or where Viola's eyes remained blindfolded, keeping her from discerning the true form of her reflection.

But Talia always remained tethered to Viola, even without a leash, in some invisible way. She ought to only mirror what Viola did, not strike out on her own in search of her own adventures and lovers, not forge her own paths, not fall in love with Inniyeth.

Viola didn't know what to say, and so she stayed silent. Eventually, Talia's sobs subsided, exhaustion overpowering her grief, even if only briefly, and Viola helped her lie down on the bed and tucked her under the sheets. She remained seated on the edge of the bed until she could feel Talia's body relax as she slipped into deep slumber.

Viola returned to the table, but the food had grown cold. She thought of ringing for Noyoni and her sisters, ask them to warm up the dishes, but realized that she too had lost her appetite. The morsels that had tasted so tantalizing mere minutes ago no longer held the ability to numb the pain of life.

No scent or flavour in the world could assuage and soften the lump of dread that now sat in the pit of her stomach, dragging her down, causing her to hunch over as if she were under the weight of an impossibly heavy burden. The prospect of imminent death had become excruciatingly painful, now that there was so much more to lose.

CHAPTER 10

SNEAK A PEEK BEFORE SHE DISAPPEARS

Viola was the first to awake the next morning. She had slept fitfully, constantly reaching out to feel for Talia beside her.

Ever since Viola and Ronin had looked into each other's eyes without a blindfold in their way, Talia had guided her to safety. Viola had merely followed the tug on the leash that had bound them. Now that Talia was fatigued, a sense of responsibility and protectiveness towards her reflection surged in Viola.

All her thoughts were of Talia that morning. Viola sat up in bed. Before she could stop herself, she reached for the knot of the blindfold behind her eyes and untied it. The cloth remained stuck to her face, glued to the raw skin on her cheekbones, and Viola had to peel it apart. It stung a little. Not a new sensation at all.

She rubbed her eyes with the heels of her palms and opened them slowly. This was probably the last time she'd see Talia and the rest of the world around her with eyes wide open.

As the light of the world outside poured into her eyes, memories began to flood her mind's eye. Memories she didn't know she possessed. Memories of the very first time she had opened her eyes.

The first time Viola had seen the world, she had been a day old. She had no memory of what or whom she had first laid her eyes on. All she could recollect was a blur. A blob. Which, in the days following her birth, took on the form of a face and a voice she came to recognize as her mother's.

Once a day, before the world stirred, before the dark night peeled itself away from the light of dawn, Viola's mother opened her blindfold and her child's, and peered into the little one's eyes.

Once a day, away from the shut eyes of the world around her, Viola's mother took a few moments to take in the sight of her daughter and hoped to imprint an image of herself on her little child's soul.

Once a day, Viola's mother sought to show her daughter what a beautiful world they lived in, even if the very act of showing and seeing put them in mortal peril.

Once a day, Viola's mother cooed to her, "Green as the deepest ocean are your eyes and mine. Take in all these sights and remember them until the end of your days."

Once a day for the first five years of her life, every morning before the rest of the household stirred, Viola untied her blindfold and opened her eyes.

Once a day, Viola looked around her to see if she could spot her mother once more, her eyes green as the leaves of the apple tree, the only eyes she had seen until she had peered into Ronin's, his blank eyes, his pupils bleached colourless owing to years of disuse. Ronin blinded by the unfamiliar harshness of bright sunlight, seeing what he shouldn't have had to see, a reflection in a land where everyone had been robbed of theirs.

Once a day, Viola saw what she ought not to have seen.

The shimmer of stars in the sky on a cold, winter morning. The tufts of breath-clouds that tumbled out of her mouth like little slivers of her soul. The vast expanse of freshly fallen snow on land; large, white sheets unmarred by human footprints.

Baby leaves in the springtime, shining with newness.

The first light of dawn breaking through the sky on a summer morning. Leaves on the trees, darkening.

She never knew her colours. She hadn't known their names. But that hadn't taken away her awe, the wonder she experienced every time she set eyes on the world around her, taking in all the sights, hungrily, greedily, devouring the way the stars winked at her and the leaves jiggled and the flowers bobbed, as if only for her. Their dance made livelier because of the attention she paid to them.

Then there were the birds and the animals. She knew them by their songs and their calls, by the way they scurried and scampered on the forest floor or up and down trees, or by the way they flapped their wings.

Robins, who woke her up before daybreak in the summer. Blue jays. Cardinals. The male, bold and bright, unabashedly loud in his calls. The female, cleverly camouflaged to keep predators away from her eggs and babies. Squirrels that ran headfirst down trees without fear of falling.

The way the leaves changed in autumn, turning the colour of fire or the colour of roses, and eventually bid farewell to the branches they had clung to all spring and summer. The way they crunched under her feet.

Oh, for a few brief moments in the morning Viola held the world in her eyes, and for the rest of the day and night, she held all of it in her heart, the blindfold back on her eyes, keeping all the images of the world she had seen pressed within her eyes and on her soul so they wouldn't seep out and escape.

Viola never attempted to see anyone other than her mother in those brief morning moments of sight. And then her parents had perished when she was five years old. In an accident, she was told. Since then, Viola had never felt the need to see anything or anyone in the world outside, until Ronin had come along.

But this morning, she wanted to see Talia, knowing it may well be the last time she'd behold her sister, her reflection, her lifelong companion.

She blinked her eyes slowly and repeatedly to habituate herself to the flickering light from the candles in the room. The swish of her long eyelashes was almost inaudible to her keen ears.

Talia lay beside her, curled up like a foetus in a womb. If this was the day they were destined to die, Viola would go to the guillotine with the image of her mother and of her reflection seared on the inside of her eyelids. She untied Talia's blindfold gently, hoping to not wake her.

There was something vulnerable about Talia. Unexposed to the sun, the skin around her eyes was paler than the rest of her face. A special kind of mark that all Parinaryans had been branded with.

Viola swept Talia's locks away from her face. An unveiling.

An unmasking. To get a clearer look at the one being she held dear.

Her act reminded her of the way her mother used to sweep Viola's curly locks away from her forehead and her eyes. "There, now I see you, now you see me," her mother would say. Tears sprang from Viola's eyes at the memory and spilled on Talia's cheek.

Talia smiled. Eyes still shut, she reached out with a hand and felt for Viola. Viola grasped Talia's hand in hers and pressed it to her damp cheek. Talia's smile slipped into a frown, and she opened her eyes.

In that instant, she disappeared. Her hand slipped out of Viola's, who was left clutching a fistful of empty air.

"Talia," she screamed.

"Viola," a thousand voices of Talia hollered in response.

Viola looked around, and there was Talia. One instance of her, in the big, gold-framed mirror that hung on the wall opposite the bed.

Talia called out again, and her fear-stricken faces, too many of them to count, peered out at Viola.

From the mirror beside the bed. From the shiny, reflective surfaces of the countless sequins embroidered into every visible piece of textile in the room. Curtains. Upholstery.

From the innumerable crystals that clinked in the chandelier far above the bed, reflecting Viola's face back at her, mimicking her panic, her terror, those tiny, exquisite, transparent pieces trembling from the force of Talia's cries of anguish erupting from within them.

From the forks and spoons and the gleaming utensils that held last evening's dinner, a lavish meal that Viola had left unfinished.

From the brass knob on the door and the gold plating that adorned the frames that set the boundaries of everything in this room. Paintings. Doorways. Crown embellishments on the ceiling.

Everywhere Viola looked, Talia's face looked back at her and cried for help. Begged to be released.

In that instant, Viola knew what insanity had driven Queen Sahana of Parinara to destroy every mirror, every reflective surface she came across.

Seized by an inexplicable rage, Viola grabbed the chair she had sat upon at mealtime last evening, a heavy object padded with the fluffiest of cottons and dressed in the finest of silks. With a scream loud enough to shatter glass, she hurled it at the mirror on the wall facing the bed. Talia in the mirror splintered into a thousand selves, each screaming from the thousand shards of glass that now lay on the floor.

The commotion did not go unnoticed. The door to the room flung open, letting in a whoosh of air.

The guards were upon Viola in an instant, but she spun around and stared at them with wild eyes, their green so pale they appeared completely white at first glance.

Her seemingly empty gaze, its power preserved by almost a lifetime of blindness, stopped them in their tracks.

The ones unfortunate enough to look into her eyes fell down unconscious, as if struck by lightning, shocked out of their wits at the sight of those ghostly eyes, quite like the very first Anansian guard who had had the misfortune of peering into Talia's eyes.

Those who were far behind enough to witness Viola's unsettling gaze without being subdued by it turned around to alert the others.

Someone shouted for a veil. Soon a black shroud was passed from one guard to the other down the long corridor that led to the room where Viola and Talia had been accommodated.

The guards closest to the room and still on their feet unravelled the black fabric and held it up in front of them like a shield. Like a veil between them and Viola.

Crouching and shivering behind the garment, they stepped forward, slowly, praying silently for the thick, opaque piece of fabric to shield them from the wrath of a raging Parinaryan.

After all, their Queen had attempted to kill the ruler of Anansia, even if it was only a long time ago. Who knew what kind of insanity had established itself in the minds and hearts of her subjects when she stole their sight from them?

They need not have feared, for Viola had no intention of hurting any of them. All she was intent on doing was destroying every surface that reflected Talia's face of agony back at her.

At the king's court, Talia had warned Viola to not open her blindfold. She had known of the consequences that awaited them if Viola gave in to that impulse of hers. Only, Viola had failed to pay heed.

When the guards pounced upon her and covered her face with the black weapon they wielded, a seemingly harmless length of cloth, dark and thick enough to not let much light escape through its threads, Viola offered no resistance. No blindfold would bring Talia back now. Not for as long as there were mirrors and other reflective surfaces in which she'd remain trapped.

Like a prisoner being led to the gallows, Viola was escorted out of the room with the black cloth covering her face and neck, and her hands tied behind her back. Tears streamed down her eyes. The cloth covering her face quickly became damp and stuck to her cheeks.

"Where is Talia?" A voice whispered into her ear.

Inniyeth! The concern for Talia in his gentle voice made Viola sob harder.

"Gone," she whispered between sobs. The word came out strangulated. Twisted and choked. Deformed by her emotions.

Her utterance only earned her a merciless shove and a yell of "Quiet!" from another guard.

The guards led her to the king's court. Viola paid little attention to the path they were taking. Her senses were numb. The presence of scents and sounds grated on her nerves. All she could sense was the heaviness in her heart, which made her feel it was impossible to take another step. But walk she did, putting one step ahead of another. It was only when she was brought to a halt and pushed to the ground, where she fell prostrate, that she recognized the cool marble that had risen to meet her temple.

Someone pulled her up gently so she could sit a little upright. Inniyeth, she knew without doubt.

Would he be punished for this little act of mercy? But no, they were in Anansia, a land known for its clemency and kindness.

Yet, her shoulders sagged, and the weight in her heart threatened to pull her towards the floor. For Inniyeth's sake, for Talia's sake, she mustered all her strength and pulled her spine erect. The very act strengthened her will.

"Where is your sister?" King Alahaid's voice boomed throughout the durbar. The loudness of his voice suggested to her that even in Anansia, kindness could be withheld when the situation demanded.

Think, Viola said to herself. *What would Talia do?*

But that was the wrong question. For there was no Talia now. So the only question to be asked and answered was: what will Viola do?

The answer that came to her was simple. And obvious.

"Forgive me, my Lord," Viola bowed her head, while still keeping her spine erect as best as she could with her hands cuffed behind her back. Her voice had gone hoarse, strained from the screams that had emerged from her throat back in the room where she had lost Talia. Her throat ached but she pressed on. "Forgive me, my Lord, but Talia is not my sister. She is my reflection."

A collective gasp went around the court.

"Anansia is the land of the kind, the kingdom of the large-hearted, but no duplicity is tolerated here," King Alahaid spoke with a calmness that failed to conceal his fury.

"Please, my Lord," Viola cried. "We meant no deceit. Please allow me to explain."

The King made a gesture with a wave of his arm and a grunt that could have meant anything. *Take her away. Throw her at the mercy of Queen Sahana.*

But Viola decided to interpret it as assent. Even if she were mistaken, she'd be forgiven for her misinterpretation; she was blindfolded after all. Having convinced herself thus, she launched into a monologue, trying not to pause for breath too often, lest she be interrupted and deprived of the opportunity to save herself and Talia.

She spun a true tale of a queen who had once been rejected, first by a king, then by a Seer, and then by a mirror.

It was this last rejection that was her undoing. A rejection of herself by her own self. And she had severed her true reflection from herself. Demolished the only avenue available to look into her own soul. A fate that had to be borne by her subjects for decades to come.

Viola next spun a true tale of a little girl whose mother sought to give her little glimpses of the world beyond, and in so doing inadvertently ensured her true self would not be separated from her. Thus, Talia had been born. A reflection in a land of no reflection. A personification of truth in a land where no one had the sight to behold her. That was the only place Talia could survive.

Until Viola had taken up a dare—and no, the boy had not been worth it, Your Highness—and she and Talia had had to run away to ensure their survival.

At first, Viola had assumed she was the only one in danger. Turned out it was Talia's survival that had been in question all along. It was Talia's survival that had hung in the balance ever since she had come into existence.

But Viola had learnt of this truth only on the shores of the lake of Anansia, where she and Talia had dared to remove their blindfolds and look into each other's eyes for the first time.

Talia's eyes, devoid of pupils at first, vast milky oceans of nothingness. But they had turned a vivid green when the water of the lake had devoured her, and welcomed her back to her true abode.

"You have green eyes?" King Alahaid interrupted.

"I … I … beg … Forgive me … I beg your pardon, my Lord?" Viola stuttered, startled back into the present moment from her reminiscences, having forgotten for an instant that there was an audience to her story, hanging on to her every word.

"Remove the mask from her face," the king commanded.

"Please, my Lord," Viola cried out, "my sight will cause needless harm. They present too ghastly a sight to bear."

The king must have seen reason, for no guard ventured to peel the fabric from Viola's face.

"Why do you claim to have green eyes?" King Alahaid asked.

"I … It is what my reflection in the lake showed me, Your Highness," Viola said. She couldn't fathom why this detail would bother him so.

"How is it possible that you, who has had little opportunity since birth to take in the sights of the world around you, can distinguish one colour from another?"

King Alahaid was not only merciful but also intelligent, Viola realized. It strengthened her resolve to continue to speak the truth and nothing but the truth, for the good king of Anansia deserved nothing but the words of her truest self.

She spun yet another true tale of how the children of Anansia grew up learning that the grass was green and the sky was blue on a sunny summer's day, that the leaves of fruit-laden trees were green and a thunderstorm was grey and sombre.

Why then had Talia declared to the first guard they had met in the apple orchard that her eyes were golden and shiny? It was a dilemma that had nagged Viola and she stumbled over the words she employed to tell her story. Her stumbling was evident to none but the very perceptive King of Anansia. Before he could question or chastise her, she presented to him the conundrum that troubled her. She didn't know why she had green eyes.

"It is the people of Anansia who have green eyes," King Alahaid said. "The people of Parinara were long renowned for their golden eyes, said to shine like the sun on a cool day in autumn, gentle and warm, not piercingly sharp nor blinding. Few remember such a detail now, for so long have your people lived without the gift of sight."

"But my mother had green eyes too," Viola said, the truth of her sentence dawning upon her only as she said it aloud. *Green as the deepest ocean are your eyes and mine.* Her mother's words rang in her ears, loud and clear like a skylark's song. *Take in all these sights and remember them until the end of your days.*

The silence in the court was louder than any sound that must have reverberated between those decorated walls. The lively sounds of performers, singing and dancing and telling stories to entertain the King and his court. The plaintive cries of those seeking justice. The sombre and sincere debates among the courtiers over the future of Anansia. The echoes and remnants of every word spoken in this space since it was built and inhabited.

"If that is true, then you belong to Anansia," King Alahaid said. "Your mother too must have been from this land."

The king's proclamation brought sweet relief to Viola. Alongside a burst of confusion.

Was her mother from Anansia? How could that be?

But also, how could it not be? It explained perfectly how Viola knew the story of Queen Sahana's stealth attack on Anansia when King Alahaid was a newborn. Viola had known a story that only Anansians had the privilege of knowing, because she too was one of them.

It all made sense now. Her mother's daring act of regularly removing her daughter's blindfold in a land where such a deed was punishable by death. No Anansian would have wanted her only daughter to grow up completely sightless. No Anansian would have wanted to subject her only child to the cruel laws of Parinara.

Did this mean Viola was pardoned? Did this mean she wouldn't have to return to Parinara? But if she stayed back in Anansia, would she remain captive for the rest of her life? And what about Talia? All these questions trembled on Viola's lips, but she dared not pose them aloud, fearful that the answers may not be the ones she hoped for.

"But first the veracity of your claims must be determined," the King of Anansia continued. "A visit to Queen Sahana of Parinara is in order. We leave immediately."

CHAPTER 11
THE WAY BACK HOME

Viola, blindfolded once more with a strip of cloth and not the black shroud that had covered her face, found the journey back to Parinara relatively anticlimactic compared with the rather dramatic fashion in which she and Talia had left their homeland.

It wasn't death itself that she feared but this period of waiting, these hours and minutes leading up to the final moments of her life, that kept her restless. Her unease agitated her horse too, and Inniyeth spent most of the journey travelling beside her, keeping quiet—she was not Talia after all—and focussed only on keeping her horse calm and in check.

Only once did he lean towards her, his armour clinking loud enough to attract her attention, and whispered, "Will Talia never come back?"

Viola had been unable to respond at first. It was a question she had asked herself countless times ever since Talia had been sucked into the innumerable glittering surfaces of glass and crystal that adorned the room at the palace where they had been held captive for a brief night. "I don't know," she had said eventually. Inniyeth had drawn back, the gap between them filled with the heavy cloud of his disappointment and her helplessness.

A resolute silence marked the remainder of the journey. It was noon but the autumn sun refused to reach the heights it had scaled in the sky only a month ago, preferring instead to hang closer to the ground for a clearer view of what was about to transpire. Even the birds were quiet. Only a distant, feeble trill travelled occasionally over the treetops.

The constant clatter of the horses' hoofs kept her on edge, a constant reminder that they were speeding towards Parinara. It had taken her and Talia two days and two nights to reach Anansia. The horses needed barely more than half a day to bring her back to the land she had fled from.

It wasn't until they reached the boundary that separated Anansia from Parinara that Viola heard another human being speak.

"Halt!" a guard of Parinara commanded. "Who are you? What brings you to the land of Parinara?"

"King Alahaid of Anansia seeks an audience with Queen Sahana of Parinara," a guard of Anansia responded. "We come in peace."

The voices that spoke were so distant it occurred to Viola for the first time that King Alahaid must have brought a sizeable force with him. She had been so lost in her thoughts of Talia and the fate that lay in store for her at Parinara that she had missed *seeing* what had been going on around her.

Had the King of Anansia come with the intention of waging war on Parinara? Would she serve as the pawn who'd be sacrificed for the greater good or some such grand vision? But the captain of the guards of Anansia had said they had arrived in peace. Besides, thus far he had not breathed a word of the Parinaryan in their midst.

"Your Highness, forgive us but we must send word to the queen before we can permit you entry into Parinara."

Now that Viola was straining to grasp the words, she recognized the voice. It sent a tremor of fear down her spine. It was one of the guards of Parinara who had pursued Viola and Talia into the woods. He'd be delighted to drag Viola by the hair and have her beheaded with one swift slash of his sword, whether Queen Sahana willed it or not. Vengeance for the harm Viola and Talia had caused his captain, his comrades, and their horses.

King Alahaid must have agreed to the guard's request for the soldiers around Viola dismounted and led their horses away from the path to tie them to trees. Inniyeth helped Viola dismount and led her horse away. She followed him, not wanting to be left behind. It wasn't as if the guards of Parinara could *see* her, but they were less likely to discern her scent or her soft footfall if all these attributes of her being were muffled by the platoon around her.

It was early evening, Viola could tell from the way the breeze began to grow chillier and the light outside her blindfold grew dimmer and softer. Inniyeth handed her a bowl of something warm—stew, she realized upon taking a sip—and placed a loaf of bread in her hand. He sat beside her, and soon a few other guards joined them.

All around her, the guards formed little groups and settled down for a meal, their first since they had set forth from Anansia that morning. They joked and teased, traded gossip, talked about their families.

Someone mentioned King Janaheed, and it was only then

that Viola remembered with a shock that King Alahaid was still in mourning for his father. Yet he had not let his grief stand in the way of dispensing his duties towards his people.

There was a conviviality that reminded Viola of Talia. Not that she had forgotten her in the first place. But she missed the easy, honest way in which she and Talia could tell each other whatever arose in their hearts and minds. Without guile. Without pretence.

A fire was kindled. And then another. And yet another. One roared to life close to Viola. An occasional warmth drifted her way when the breeze coaxed and stirred the fire and the flames leaned towards her, close enough to keep her warm without touching her.

"Why did Talia disappear?"

Viola looked up in the direction the question had come from. It had been posed to her, she was certain of that. But it hadn't been Inniyeth. Another guard had inquired. Perhaps, he hadn't been in court when Viola had narrated her tale to the King of Anansia. One from the lower ranks, perhaps.

"Because she was not a real person, like you or I," Viola said. "She was only a reflection. And when I opened my eyes in a room that held a mirror, she was pulled back into it. The place where she truly belongs."

"How could you say that?" The hurt and accusation in Inniyeth's voice startled Viola. "She is as real as any of us here. She thinks. She feels. She hurts. She imagines. And she makes no effort to conceal any of that. All of that makes her real."

Shame warmed up Viola's cheeks and burnt her eyes. She wanted to tug at her blindfold and discard it to let the heat from her eyes dissipate into the air around her. "You are right," she said. "She merely exists on the other side of a mirror, but that doesn't make her any less real than the rest of us."

The conversation around her moved on to other topics, and Viola lapsed into silence with relief.

Inniyeth had known Talia for less than a day, yet he had accorded her a place in his heart and in this universe. His acknowledgement of her, of who she was, had made her real in his eyes.

Viola had known Talia all her life in many ways, without quite knowing her in only one other way. Yet, all it had taken was that one unknown for her to dismiss her lifelong companion as unreal. Insubstantial.

"Do you feel betrayed?" Inniyeth asked.

That was the word. Betrayal. "Yes." Viola clutched at the word as if it were the answer to all her conundrums. "Yes, yes," she said again and again. "To know someone for a lifetime, only to realize that you never knew them at all."

"If that is what ails you," he said, "then let me assure you of this. We can never truly know the other, no matter how many lifetimes we may have had the good fortune of spending with each other. Besides, Talia is not the only one who kept a secret from you. Even your mother hid her true origins from you. Has it occurred to you that they might have acted solely in your interest? To safeguard you? Knowledge is not always a wieldy tool. Often, ignorance serves us better."

Inniyeth's wise words were like a balm to Viola's aching heart. Her face broke into a smile. She had never perceived the situation that way. But now that Inniyeth had shown her a different point of view, a glimpse of what may have truly motivated her mother and Talia to do what they did, Viola no longer felt the need to cling to the weight that had pressed upon her heart for two days and a night, ever since Talia had revealed to her who she truly was. Suddenly she found that she could breathe easily.

She took in a deep breath, the air of Anansia mingled with that of Parinara. No boundary between the two kingdoms could separate the air and the sky. No line of demarcation could be drawn across the sky to mirror the one that was scratched on the face of the land to keep clouds from drifting and birds from flying from one kingdom to another. Nothing could prevent the trees growing on the land of one ruler from dropping their shade on the land belonging to the other.

On the breeze that floated from Parinara towards Anansia, Viola detected the faint scent of roses and lavender. A whiff of an exotic perfume. She knew of only one person whose being bloomed with such a scent. She gasped.

"What is it?" Inniyeth asked.

"The Queen! She has arrived."

CHAPTER 12

A CRISIS OF IDENTITY

"The Queen is coming," Viola whispered, worried that the breeze would choose this instant to change course and drag the sound of her voice up to Queen Sahana and the guards of Anansia.

Inniyeth wasted no time in alerting the captain, who informed King Alahaid of this development. With silent efficiency, the guards jumped up, cleared away the remnants of their meal, and put out the fires they had huddled around.

They then untied their horses, mounted them, and assembled themselves in neat rows behind their king. They were keeping themselves open to the possibility of peaceful talks but also bracing themselves for war. Inniyeth helped Viola up on her horse and she too was taken back to her place in the regiment. It was as if the past hour or two of camaraderie had not transpired.

Images of light flickered in front of her eyes and the thick aroma of oil filled the air around them. The guards had lit lanterns. Night had fallen, Viola realized, having missed the disappearance of the sun and his light behind the horizon.

"My condolences, King Alahaid." Queen Sahana's voice rang through the night, loud and clear, entirely devoid of emotion. Only two days and a night had transpired since King Janaheed had passed away. Yet so much had taken place in the interim.

"I am grateful for your commiserations, Queen Sahana," the King of Anansia replied.

"What brings you here?" she asked, wasting no time.

"It is a matter that requires some deliberation."

"I'm afraid I cannot invite you and your army into our land, Alahaid, if that is what you ask. Parinara is the land of no reflection. The jewels on your crown, the steel of your armour, the shine of your sword, the world you hold in your eyes, none of these are conducive to Parinaryans. If any of my people were to set eyes on their reflection, they would go stark raving mad."

"I have seen it for myself," King Alahaid said.

There was a pause in which Viola wished the sky would fall upon them or the earth would open up under her feet and swallow her and then seal itself close again, obliterating her from existence in one fell swoop.

Nothing of the sort happened. What happened instead was this. Inniyeth dismounted, then helped Viola climb down from her horse. He held her by the elbow and led her on foot towards Parinara. Viola tried to walk with firm steps but her legs kept threatening to give way under her. Inniyeth did not offer her his arm. He only kept nudging her towards her unavoidable fate.

"Your Majesty," he said, when they came to a halt.

Viola couldn't tell if Inniyeth had addressed King Alahaid or Queen Sahana. The scent of mixed roses and lavender was too strong to deny the fact that Viola stood in front of her queen.

Viola curtsied too. "Your Majesty," she whispered. The words came out as a croak. A strangled address.

One of the guards of Parinara spoke in a low tone to Queen Sahana. His words presented themselves as muffled whispers to King Alahaid and the other Anansians, but every Parinaryan who stood at the border between the two kingdoms heard their new captain inform their queen that the girl who had spoken was the traitor they had pursued and lost in the woods.

"Ah!" Queen Sahana said. Not even the slightest tremor marred her voice. "I take it you have come to return our fugitive to us, Alahaid. Your honesty and sense of justice are commendable. Grief has not clouded your mind. You will make a better ruler than your father. Now, if you please, you may hand over the traitor to our captain, newly appointed but our most capable yet, and he will see to it that justice is done. I must take your leave now."

Without waiting for a response from King Alahaid, the queen tugged at her horse's reins and nudged it to turn around.

"Your fugitive is an Anansian," King Alahaid called out. "She is not subject to the laws of Parinara."

Moments stretched into eternity as the queen turned around to face them again. "And how do you know this? Have you committed the folly of looking into her eyes?" The sarcasm in her voice was undeniable.

But King Alahaid refused to be flustered. "I was hoping you could offer us assistance in establishing the veracity of her claims," he said without inflection.

"Impossible!" Queen Sahana said without hesitation. "Parinara is a land of no reflection. Under no circumstances can I permit anyone in this land to remove their blindfold to look into the eyes of another. It is a crime punishable by death. A crime this fugitive is guilty of. Off to the guillotine with her!"

The guards of Parinara moved a step towards the Anansian troops who responded by promptly brandishing their weapons and positioning themselves between their enemy and their king.

"Queen Sahana!" King Alahaid said, his voice stern and determined. He was no longer the prince whose life had been nearly snuffed out by the queen he addressed. He was now a king, a ruler who had to make tough decisions on the merit of justice whether or not his former assailant would be displeased. "Viola is not beholden to Parinara. On the contrary, she is an Anansian who has been subjected to the cruel laws of Parinara for all fifteen years of her life."

"What is your objective in bringing her here then and demanding an audience with me?"

"Because her claims of having eyes as green as the deepest ocean remain unverified."

When Queen Sahana did not reply, King Alahaid pressed on. "I beseech you to not end this girl's life in haste. If, upon her death, she is revealed to have been an Anansian, war between our kingdoms will be inevitable. It is not an eventuality I am in favour of."

Two thoughts stirred in Viola's mind at that moment. It occurred to her that despite her bravado, Queen Sahana might not be keen to embark on a war with Anansia. The troops of Parinara were just as adept in the use of arms as the soldiers of any other kingdom, but they had never been to war blindfolded. The last war had taken place more than half a century ago. Long before the Queen was born. Long before Parinaryans had had to learn how to live without vision.

Besides, it was one thing to be able to tell from the mere whoosh of a blade when it might strike you and duck or thwart the blow when there were only a handful of opponents to combat.

But it was quite another feat altogether to be able to exhibit such deftness amid the din of a war with the clash and clang of a thousand swords, the screams of a thousand comrades being wounded or killed, and the sound of your own thoughts and fear clamouring for attention in your head and drowning out every other sound outside.

The army of Parinara was ill-equipped for war, Viola concluded. King Alahaid must have known this long before they had set forth from Anansia, where the ashes of his late father remained in a sacred urn, waiting to be dispersed into the soil of the land he had ruled well and for long.

The other thought that rose in Viola's mind was that King Alahaid had so far made no mention of Talia. But surely the Parinaryan guard who had chased Viola and Talia, the guard who was now the new captain, must remember that he and his comrades had chased two young women, not one, in the woods. Viola stopped the thought in its tracks, afraid that its very existence might kindle the new captain's memory of Talia.

"Neither am I," Queen Sahana said at last. "I am pleased to see you follow in your late father's footsteps. Peace before war. But you demand the impossible of me. How could we possibly verify what this girl claims? It is a cardinal sin in Parinara to remove our blindfolds."

"I invite you to step over into the land of Anansia," King Alahaid said. "Here you may remove your blindfold and look into the eyes of Viola."

"I haven't once opened my eyes since the day I put on my blindfold," Queen Sahana said. "My vision will terrify everyone into shock and insanity. The girl will not survive the ordeal. Neither will any of you."

"We will blindfold ourselves and look away," King Alahaid suggested. "We will encase ourselves from neck to toe in black shrouds so that none of our metals or crystals would have the audacity to reflect your being."

While Queen Sahana deliberated with herself, weighing the relative merits and demerits of King Alahaid's suggestion, countless thoughts swirled and clashed in Viola's mind.

The queen would look into her eyes. If, as the queen claimed, she hadn't opened her eyes even once in three decades, who knows how ghastly they appeared now? Would Viola die from shock?

Besides, one look into Viola's eyes and the queen would discern immediately that Viola hadn't broken the law of the land only once. It would be evident that she had transgressed the law far too many times to count.

"Very well, then," Queen Sahana's voice sliced through Viola's thoughts. "I shall oblige you on this occasion, Alahaid. Your late father spared the life of an errant Parinaryan decades ago. If this girl here is truly an Anansian, I gladly lend you my assistance in uncovering the truth. I shall, however, not be held responsible for any undesirable effect my vision may have on her or on you and your troops. Promise me you will not seek vengeance on Parinara for any fatalities you may suffer tonight."

"We place our lives in your trust, Queen Sahana," King Alahaid said, "fully cognisant of the assurance that cannot be given."

At his gesture, the king and every one of his guards stepped several paces behind. They covered themselves in dark shrouds and tied blindfolds around their eyes and their horses' eyes too.

Viola stood where she was, trembling. Ripples of fear exploded through every part of her and rattled her very being. She clasped her hands in front of her to keep them from shaking. In the hushed silence that followed, every sound was amplified a thousand times.

Queen Sahana dismounted from her horse and landed on her feet with a soft thud that sounded like the splintering of wood to Viola. Every step that Queen Sahana took towards her sounded like the thud of a hammer on a nail. The crunch of the leaves under the queen's boots were like the splat of a little critter's body run over by a carriage.

Viola put her hands over her ears, but it helped little. All her life she had relied on her sense of hearing to avoid obstacles and dangers. This very skill threatened to kill her now before the queen's gaze could.

Queen Sahana stopped no closer than three feet away from her, Viola could tell from the sound of her breath and the intense scent of her perfume. It held an undertone of jasmine that Viola had not detected earlier.

"Take off your blindfold," the queen commanded.

Viola stood still. Her hands hung by her sides like dead lumps of lead, too heavy for her to lift them up to her face. Her fingers were too rigid to execute the intricate task of untying a knot.

"I will not repeat my command," the queen hissed. And, in a whisper so soft that only Viola could hear, she added, "If you fail to do what is demanded of you, you will pay with your life right now, you traitor."

These words of the queen had certainly not fallen on the ears of King Alahaid and his men who were several yards away from them. There was no one in Viola's vicinity who could help her should Queen Sahana decide to brandish a bejewelled knife and plunge it into Viola's heart. King Alahaid may well declare war against Parinara but it would be too late for Viola by then. No amount of bloodshed would bring her back to life.

Viola didn't trust the queen but she saw no other alternative. She untied her blindfold and dropped the piece of cloth, made of the finest silk she had ever wrapped around her eyes, at the queen's feet.

She stood with her eyes shut tight, determined to not open them. She clasped her hands in front of her once more and bowed her head as if in prayer, hoping that the last thing she'd see in this beautiful world would not be Queen Sahana but her mother's face, sweet and gentle with eyes as green as the deepest ocean.

"Anansians," Queen Sahana said, her voice booming like thunder, "guard your sight the way you'd guard your lives. Parinaryans, you have nothing to fear. Your blindfolds will shield you from all harm, as they always have. No matter what you perceive outside closed eyes, no matter what you hear, dare not remove your blindfolds, dare not open your eyes. Dare not approach us unless you hear my command."

Viola heard the swish of one swatch of fabric sliding

against another as the queen tugged at the knot on the back of her head.

Then came the feathery whoosh of silken cloth falling through the air and settling down upon the ground like dust.

A breath later, the world exploded.

CHAPTER 13

THE TRUTH, AT LAST

First, there came the light. Which Viola hadn't expected. She felt herself bathed in a bright light. Had three decades of disuse lent some magical ability to the queen's sight?

Viola put her arms up to shield her eyes from the glare. Even if she had wanted to open her eyes, she couldn't have. The explosion of light from the queen's eyes made Viola squeeze her own eyes shut even more.

Then came the sound. The wrath of Queen Sahana. "Open your eyes!" she yelled, when she had opened hers and seen Viola's still shut. Viola tumbled back involuntarily, her arms still over her face. The queen's booming voice pushed her back as if it were a tangible force whipping her off her feet.

Finally came the scream. Only, it didn't come from Viola's mouth but from the queen's.

The next instant, everything was gone. The light. The sound. The scream. Everything ceased. Like a life snuffed out.

~

Viola opened her eyes slowly, wary of letting her gaze fall upon any Anansian who may have foolishly removed their blindfold. There was always at least one person who flouted the rules. She ought to know that very well. She was one of their kind.

The night shimmered and danced in front of her. She rubbed her eyes to see more clearly. Light from the lanterns the Anansian guards had lit earlier flickered and made silhouettes and night shadows dance alongside.

It took her another moment to realize that Queen Sahana was gone. In her place genuflected a person, cocooned like a black egg. His body was shrouded in black cloth. A black blindfold covered his eyes. An Anansian, then. In his hand, he held an object. Viola couldn't see what it was, as he knelt with his back to her.

To her left, King Alahaid and his men stood with their backs to her, facing away, just as Queen Sahana had instructed in no unclear terms. Shrouded and blindfolded, they appeared like young trees wrapped in jute for the winter.

To her right, the guards of Parinara stood facing her, their vision still impaired by their blindfolds but all their other senses on high alert.

"Your Highness?" the captain of Parinara inquired.

"She wasn't real." The person kneeling in front of Viola rose and turned around to face her.

"Inniyeth?" Viola recognized his voice.

"She was merely a reflection." Inniyeth's lips wobbled.

"What are you talking about?"

Inniyeth did not reply but simply presented the object he held in his hand. A flat thing. Sharp edges that met at pointy corners. Like a shard. Viola took it in her hand and held it up. In the pale light of the moon, she saw herself in the object.

"A mirror?"

Shocked at what she saw in her hand, she dropped it. Even with his blindfold on, Inniyeth was quick to catch it in his gloved hand.

Viola peered into the mirror again as Inniyeth held it up for her. A pair of green eyes peered back at her.

"Viola," the face called out.

"Talia?"

Talia's face lit up with a smile.

"It's you, isn't it?" Viola shrieked. "It's you. It's you." She was so excited at the sight of Talia that she barely registered the hazy figure that lurked in the background.

In that instant, the mirror was yanked out of Inniyeth's hand. Viola looked up. The captain of the guards of Parinara towered over them. "What's all the commotion about? Where's our queen?" he demanded.

His voice brought the Anansians rushing towards where Inniyeth and Viola stood, where Queen Sahana had stood moments ago. The black shrouds and blindfolds they discarded in their haste covered the ground in their wake and made it appear charred.

"What's going on?" King Alahaid asked.

"Queen Sahana was an illusion," Inniyeth said.

A colossal wave of rage surged in the heart of the Parinaryan captain. He dropped the shard to the ground, drew his sword from his scabbard, raised it high above his head, and brought it down on Inniyeth with a howl of fury.

"No!" With a scream, Viola hurled herself at Inniyeth and sent the two of them crashing to the ground. The blade sliced the skin on her back, from the dip between her shoulder blades down to her waist. Skin split noiselessly. For a brief instant, Viola wondered why it didn't hurt. Even before she could complete her thought, pain exploded through her being and fragmented it. An instant later, there was nothing left to feel.

Spurred by Viola's cry of agony, the brave men of Anansia drew their swords from their sheaths but their blindfolds impeded them severely. Unafraid of succumbing to Viola's gaze, they peeled away their blindfolds and charged towards the Parinaryans.

Swords struck and clanged. Cries of the wounded pierced the air. Although the Anansian army had come to expect nothing but the most skillful attack from the Parinaryan guards, they were still surprised at the level of expertise the blindfolded men of Parinara displayed. Their lack of vision was more an advantage than an impediment.

Yet, it didn't take long for King Alahaid's army to disarm the Parinaryan guards and capture them as prisoners of war. Even in war, the soldiers of Anansia did not seek to kill.

"Parinaryans," King Alahaid hollered when all of Queen Sahana's guards were brought to their knees, their arms tied behind their backs. "Where is your Queen?"

"Here." Inniyeth's voice came as a whimper. He was buried under Viola. She had fallen face down on him. Her head was on his chest. She was gravely injured, it was evident from the warm stickiness of the blood that gushed from her back.

Her small, lithe body had somehow protected him more than his armour of steel could. He pulled off his blindfold and pointed to the mirror that lay beside them, a little out of reach, without moving the rest of his body, afraid to disturb Viola. The slightest movement could aggravate her wounds.

The captain of the Anansian guards knelt beside Inniyeth and took the mirror from the ground, which he passed on to King Alahaid. Inniyeth's comrades turned Viola to her side.

"Gently," Inniyeth urged. But his concern was futile. No cry of pain escaped her lips when his comrades moved her. They encountered no resistance as they laid her on her back.

Inniyeth pulled himself up and sat on his haunches beside her. The girl who had saved his life by giving up her own.

Did her vision still have the power to hurt? Inniyeth refused to entertain that question. It was the least he could do for her.

He gestured for a lantern. When he received one, he shone its light on her face. Her eyes were wide open, as if the blow had startled her. Green as the deepest ocean were her pupils.

"Anansian," Inniyeth whispered.

His captain and his comrades too looked into Viola's eyes in a final gesture of gratitude and respect. Anansian, Anansian, they all murmured. Like a prayer.

King Alahaid knelt beside the young woman's corpse. In the yellow light of the lantern, the green of her eyes shone and sparkled like emeralds.

The skin around her eyes and on her temples was paler than elsewhere on her face. It was an affliction that only Parinaryans bore, their blindfolds keeping out the light of the sun for all their lives. For almost all their lives.

How had an Anansian been born in the land of Parinara? Viola's mother had hailed from Anansia with eyes green as the deepest ocean. It must have been the father then, unfortunate enough to be bound to the rules of Parinara.

"Viola?" A voice called from the shard of mirror that King Alahaid still gripped in his hand. The king turned the mirror so that it faced Viola. A cry of anguish erupted from the mirror. It rent the night around them and made the stars wobble.

In that instant, Viola's spirit rose from her body. A white orb of light, smaller than a fist, rose from her heart. Bouncing and bobbing. A bauble of life. It floated towards the mirror and disappeared into it.

CHAPTER 14

INSIDE THE MIRROR

Two young women in the mirror.

They could be mistaken for twins.

But closer than siblings they were.

"What will happen to Parinara now?" Viola whispered. No blindfold covered her eyes.

"Our land got lucky," Talia said. Her eyes now were as green as Viola's. "They couldn't have found a better ruler than King Alahaid."

"It's still hard to believe that Parinara was ruled all these years by a mere … a mere what? Reflection? Illusion? It's unfathomable. How could such a thing have even happened?"

"I've been wondering too. You know what they say? That we only see what we want to see? And if we are not permitted to see anything in the first place, we'd have no choice but to believe that what we're told is the truth."

"Queen Sahana's reflection ensured no one would ever see her and no reflective surface would ever appear to wrench her out of that world and back into where she truly belonged."

Viola in the mirror looked behind her. There was nothing

but a silvery mist. "Is she still here somewhere?" she asked with a shudder.

"Even if she is, she has nothing to do with us. In the world of mirrors, we only have ourselves to reckon with. Nothing else. No one else."

Talia was right, Viola realized. Queen Sahana had been killed and her soul cast into the mirror by her own reflection, the one she hated so much it had turned against her. The one who had eradicated every reflective surface in Parinara so it wouldn't be drawn back to where it belonged. Until Inniyeth had come along and held up a mirror to the queen's eyes to reveal who she truly was.

"Will our people get used to living without their blindfolds?"

"In time, yes. Now is a good time to be a Parinaryan. Before the power of sight diminishes their other senses somewhat."

Viola smiled and leaned back against Talia. This was their home now. There wasn't much to do inside a mirror. Living in the mirror was like looking out of the window of a carriage and watching the world go by. If someone on the outside paused to peek, they only needed to be shown their truths.

The shard of mirror was now encased in a gilded frame and mounted on the tallest turret of the castle of Anansia. From up here, they had a bird's-eye view of Anansia.

Nothing was hidden from sight anymore.

The way the blue skies kissed the shimmering lake of Anansia at the horizon.

The way Anansia, whose borders now extended to include the erstwhile Parinara, was ruled by a king who knew only how to do right by his people.

The way the land and the skies colour-shifted in a day and with the seasons.

It never occurred to them to look for any other place to call home.

"You could still go, you know?" Viola once said. "Inniyeth waits for you. I'll be fine here."

"Inniyeth is a good one, yes." Talia nodded. "It was ingenious of him to brandish a mirror like that."

"He did it for you."

"I know."

"You should step out and be with him. He loves you. He put his life at risk not knowing whether his deed would rescue you or not. Surely you owe your very existence to him now?"

Talia looked into Viola's eyes. "No love in the world outside is so worthy that I would seek to sever myself from you."

And that was Viola's truth revealed to her by her own self.

~ The End ~

~

Ready for more speculative fiction tales?
Dive into the adventures of A Benevolent Goddess, who is punished
for her desire to help human beings but is unable to find salvation by
any other means.

ENJOYED THE LAND OF NO REFLECTION?

Thank you for reading *The Land of No Reflection*!

If you loved the book, I hope you will consider writing a short review—even a simple line or two—on the site where you bought the book.

Publishing is still driven by word of mouth, and when you leave a review it helps other readers decide this is a book worth reading. Thank you for your help in spreading the word.

You can also sign up to my monthly newsletter for updates on new book releases as well as heartfelt reflections on writing, reading, parenting and living the creative life.

Monthly Missives from The Dream Pedlar
https://thedreampedlar.com/newsletter

104

AUTHOR'S NOTE

Dear Reader,

I started writing this tale in response to a call for short story submissions to an anthology titled 'Mirror, Mirror on the Wall'. It must have been in the fall of 2021.

I can't remember who was seeking these submissions. I do, however, remember that it appeared on a writers' group on Facebook I was part of at the time when I was still on social media.

It was a Friday evening. I started writing the beginning of the story as it appears in this book. I vividly remember writing for about six hours before realizing that there was no way I could submit this story to the anthology. You see, there was an upper limit of 5,000 words or so and I had already typed double that and was only getting into the thick of the tale.

I had never before written anything to do with kings and queens or castles and guards, although I've read countless tales featuring them. Writing this tale has taught me two things. One, imagination truly has no bounds. Second, we are our worst critics and censors. Which is why it has taken this book two long years to find its way into your hands.

But what is it they say? Better late than never.

The theme of this story is very close to my heart. I've come to realize in recent years that we truly cannot sustain a healthy relationship with the world outside if our relationship with our own self is shaky or broken.

This is a lesson I forget very often. Thankfully, I keep coming back to this nugget of wisdom just as often.

Thank you for reading all the way. I hope you enjoyed the journey this book took you on.

We've come together so far, and I hope you would like to stay connected with me. I send out a monthly newsletter on the last Sunday of every month. Subscription is free.

You will be the first to hear of my forthcoming works. I also include updates on my writing life, book recommendations, and occasional surprises.

Thank you for staying with me this far. If you choose to accompany me further on this journey, I promise you a magical ride.

Climb aboard at https://thedreampedlar.com/newsletter!

~ Anitha Krishnan
Burlington, Ontario
2 October 2023

MORE BOOKS BY ANITHA KRISHNAN

https://thedreampedlar.com/books/

Dying Wishes

Finalist for 2023 Rakuten Kobo Emerging Writer Prize in Speculative Fiction category

A contemporary fantasy novel weaving Hindu mythology and South Indian folklore into a quest for belonging across different worlds — the World of Mortals and the World of Gods, India and Canada, the past and the present, the world outside and the one within.

Erased from Existence

A paranormal mystery in which a fifteen-year-old is erased from the memories and perception of everyone. Trapped in oblivion, she will have to unearth and reveal long-buried family secrets to escape.

A Benevolent Goddess

A story of a goddess who is punished for her desire to help human beings but is unable to find salvation by any other means.

In Search of Leo

A fantasy tale exploring the gamut of emotions that loss and grief
can stir.

The Mind Meddler

A short fantasy story on the games The Mind Meddler plays by
sneaking thoughts into people's minds, until he meets the one person
who can resist his unkind mischief.

Hello, Dreamer! Poems & Dreams

An eclectic collection of 100 short poems encompassing musings on
the universe and its mysteries, nature and human life, my secret
longings and fears, love and heartbreak, the sun and the moon, the
stars and the seas, light and shadow, and joy and nostalgia.

About the Author

Anitha Krishnan is a speculative fiction author and an award-winning poet. Her fantasy novel, *Dying Wishes*, was a finalist for the 2023 Rakuten Kobo Emerging Writer Prize in the Speculative Fiction category.

She has lived in and left pieces of her heart in many places across the world including Singapore, Australia, Canada, and most of all in her beloved birthplace, India. She presently lives in Burlington, Ontario with her husband and their cherished child.

Find more books and her blog on the writing life at
https://thedreampedlar.com.

Sign up to her monthly newsletter at
https://thedreampedlar.com/newsletter
to receive heartfelt musings, exclusive updates, book recommendations, free fiction, and more!